Kuzhali Manickavel

A COMPENDIUM OF SUPERNATURAL ENTITIES FOUND IN THE GOVERNMENT GIRLS HIGHER SECONDARY SCHOOL

ANGRY ROBOT

ANGRY ROBOT
An imprint of Watkins Media Ltd

Unit 11, Shepperton House
89-93 Shepperton Road
London N1 3DF
UK

angryrobotbooks.com
No Three Rules

An Angry Robot paperback original, 2026

Edited by Simon Spanton
Cover by Sarah O'Flaherty
Set in Meridien

ISBN 978 1 91599 886 6
Ebook ISBN 978 1 91599 887 3

Printed and bound in the United Kingdom by CPI Group (UK) Ltd, Croydon CR0 4YY

The manufacturer's authorised representative in the EU for product safety is eucomply OÜ - Pärnu mnt 139b-14, 11317 Tallinn, Estonia, hello@eucompliancepartner.com; www.eucompliancepartner.com

9 8 7 6 5 4 3 2 1

FSC
www.fsc.org
MIX
Paper | Supporting responsible forestry
FSC® C013604

For A&S

Introduction

The Government Girls Higher Secondary School—or GGHSS—is one of the most supernaturally infected places in the known and unknown world. Western concepts of the supernatural should not be used as a framework while exploring, documenting, or archiving the paranormal here; the entities of the GGHSS are decidedly unWestern, and cannot be measured by Western definitions.

The Association for Moral Upliftment and Universal Friendship (AMUUF) takes great pleasure in being the first officially recognized body to endeavour to categorize and catalogue the many supernatural entities that exist within the realm of the GGHSS. With our dynamic team of researchers, archivists, and volunteers, AMUUF has achieved great things in the area of supernatural categorization. However, the monumental task of creating this compendium has not been without its challenges. Many volunteers, particularly those who have been raised in the Western school of thought, become confused as to how to identify supernatural phenomena if they do not fall into familiar slots like "vampire", "haunted house", or "Satan". The situation is made doubly difficult by the fact that many volunteers know only one language: English. This monolingual handicap severely limits the words, sounds, and ideas they have at their disposal; however, it need not hamper them in doing their job. We have always encouraged such individuals to view absolutely everything as supernatural, and work backwards from there. For example, if one comes across a chair, one should understand that it can also be an undead carnivorous bird at rest, or a community hall haunted by paranormal mushrooms. One must never assume it is just a chair.

Even today, many of the paranormal phenomena of the GGHSS remain undocumented. It pains us to note that several entries are either incomplete or totally blank, simply because the researcher/archivist/volunteer didn't feel like completing the task at hand. For example, the entries for a number of small, deceased gods, for the Giant Scrub Typhus Mites, and for the Ammapettai Fire Lizards could have been completed quite easily. However, the Ammapettai Fire Lizards entry has nothing more than a rough description of the entity's toes, while the entry for the Giant Scrub Typhus Mites is made up of the words "The Giant Scrub Typhus Mite is...", followed by at least twenty blank pages.

This brings us to our next problem. There is a good deal of documentation in this compendium that has been entirely made up, as a "joke". While AMUUF is loath to point fingers, it cannot be denied that a majority of those accused are from our volunteer base. The task of removing these entries is a daunting one and continues to be a drain on our resources.

Despite the many challenges that we continue to face in our epic endeavour, AMUUF cordially invites you to be a part of this monumental work. Should you encounter a supernatural influence that is not listed here, feel free to make detailed notes of your experience in the pages provided at the back of this compendium. Notes should include clearly labelled diagrams, maps, lists, and bagged/sealed specimens. Please do not use ballpoint pen. Kindly include any and all discharge summaries or death certificates if applicable.

***

The bus entered the town, and instantly, Thamarai forgot where she had come from. Her old life seemed to fade away, leaving behind a vacuum that was already filling up with this new town's witchy sunlight, smoke, and relentless holiness. She had been here before, when she was younger, but all she could remember from that trip was the heat, the crowds at the temple, and the priest who had conned her family out of five hundred rupees. This town would now be home for the foreseeable future.

There was no transition period, no time to work through the shock of being unceremoniously transplanted. Thamarai settled in quickly and quietly. Her new life was not terrible, but it was lonely and insignificant, dotted with only a few special occasions that involved wearing coloured dress or eating ice cream. Her parents had gotten work in two different towns, so Thamarai had been sent to stay with an unmarried aunt, who provided her meals and slept in the hall at night. Thamarai attended the local government school for girls, as well as tuitions for maths, physics, and chemistry. She went to the temple on Fridays and watched the weekly televised Tamil movie on Sundays. Hers was an ordinary life, no different from any other local girl's life.

Thamarai did not know her aunt well, but they soon settled into a routine that Thamarai found comforting. Her aunt was brisk and plump, always talking, always moving. She would watch the Sunday evening movies with Thamarai, every so often bringing out a small treat: a bar of chocolate, a bag of chips, a packet of Maggi, and on one occasion, a small glass bottle of Coke. She was sweet and unintrusive, and Thamarai decided she mostly liked her—except for her eyes, which were always hidden under round white reflections in her thick glasses. Thamarai had never actually seen her aunt's eyes, and if she thought about this too much, it scared her.

Thamarai herself was an unremarkable girl: skinny, with good teeth and thin hair. She was not pretty, but in her new school, she often got compliments from the girls because she looked like a boy. Not like a boy play-acting as a girl; to them she seemed like an actual shy, mysterious, and violent boy. It was a quality that made girls stare at her. They would sometimes touch her cheek or shyly hold her hand. They would blush or become flustered when Thamarai smiled at them. Thamarai decided this was the best aspect of her new life. She liked to see what happened when she held a gaze for too long, or absent-mindedly touched someone and let her hand linger.

Thamarai was constantly falling in love. In school, she fell in love with sports girls, bold girls, repressed conservative girls, orthodox girls, mixed-caste girls, and homely girls. She would think about these girls all the time, looking at them covertly during class, and cringing each time one of them said or did something that shattered Thamarai's beautiful idea of her. She fell in love in an intense and alarming way that would consume her completely, and then die away after a few days.

Thamarai even fell in love with the girls who made fun of her. They laughed at the parting in her hair, which was always crooked, no matter how hard she tried to straighten it. They laughed at the fact that she never put turmeric on her face or wore bangles. They laughed at her hands, which were always covered in ink even when she hadn't touched her pen, and they laughed at her school uniform, which for some reason always smelled like kerosene.

For the most part, Thamarai liked the new town. It initially seemed harmless, like a very old house. But strange things began to happen to her. Sometimes it was just unlucky strangeness: a pig would get its head stuck in the spokes of her cycle or a family of ravens would consecutively poop on her head. Other events were inexplicable: a crowd of children who all had hands where their heads should have been had once chased her while she cycled to school. Another time, while fishing in her bag for her pen, she had repeatedly pulled out handfuls of old teeth which tried to bury themselves into her palm like they were shy. There was the young man who had grabbed her arm at the railway crossing and then dissolved into a cloud of reddish dust. Another day, she had been alone at home when she had stumbled into a wall and remained stuck inside it for the whole afternoon.

And of course there was the incident with the old woman at maths tuition, which Thamarai did not like to think about.

The very first of Thamarai's supernatural experiences took place a couple of weeks after moving, on her first day of 9th standard. There had been no room for her in the classroom, so she had been relegated to sitting on the floor in the doorway. No one spoke to her, but everyone stared at her. She looked like them, but she was clearly not one of them; she was too well-nourished to be one of these girls—these girls with their anaemia, their fluoride-stained teeth, and their holes in their hearts.

She spent most of that day looking at the empty assembly ground that stretched hopelessly in front of the classroom. She memorized the pockmarks and scratches on the wall in front of her—the one crack that looked like a horse's head, the other that looked like a laughing clown. She counted the tiny holes in the floor and the mounds of dust that lay nestled at the bottom of the door.

Feeling the stares of the girls around her, she decided to rummage through her bag like she was searching for something important. Inside was a cheap, plastic raincoat, a geometry box, her unused rough notebook, her new textbooks... and something else. She frowned as she gingerly pulled out a very old and dusty botany record notebook.

She had never seen it before. Its binding was falling apart, but somehow the book seemed to be holding itself together. Thamarai looked around her to see if someone had put it in her bag by accident. A prank maybe?

She opened the notebook and saw intricate transectional sketches. These were not the usual drawings of shoeflowers and seed germination. Some of the diagrams looked like young girls and others looked like gigantic insects. The text portions almost read like botanical entries, except that they included warnings and danger rankings.

It's just a book, she said to herself. *I am not afraid of it. I'm not afraid of anything here.* She leaned over and placed the notebook on the floor, next to the wall. Someone would eventually pick it up and deal with it

She went back to staring outside.

Sometime later, when she looked in her bag again, there was the notebook, nestled under her plastic raincoat. For the next half hour, she kept putting the notebook on the floor against the wall, and it kept reappearing in her bag when she wasn't looking.

She decided she would toss it in the drainage canal on her way home.

But after school, as she slowed her pace near the canal, someone chased her away, saying it was dangerous, and didn't she have enough sense to stay away from places like that?

No matter what she tried, she could not get rid of the notebook. It became a silent, permanent fixture in her bag.

***

There were various explanations as to why this particular town was the way it was. Some believed it was the centre of all the magnetic force in the world; that's what made it so heady, intense, and unforgiving. Others said it was the sheer number of pilgrims coming to pray at the big temple that gave the town its power. So many people, praying so hard in the same place—it was bound to have some effect. Still others said it was the weight of being so old, of being continuously inhabited for so long. Millions of people eating, drinking, loving, dying all in this one town created a great tangle of energies. The more practical explanation was that there were places like this all over the world; places where the people were singular and the weather extreme, places that were unforgettable even though there was nothing memorable about them. This town was a place you either loved or hated. There was never a middle ground.

The town attracted con men, gangsters, smugglers, the silently pious, saints on bicycles, refugees, holy women, and scientists. Families that had been here for generations slowly decayed and died. Young men and women were encouraged to leave if they could, to make a life in a city, or in some other small town; but those who were born and raised here rarely left. Mysterious luxury cars sped through the roads in the middle of the night, while numerous small, hot theatres played English soft porn movies. The native vegetables were bitter gourd, spinach, lady's fingers, snake gourd, and millets. You could buy biriyani, brain fry, and country liquor under bridges, and you could get lost in the tiny bus stand. It was not strange to see dead bodies lying for hours on the railway tracks or at bus stops, waiting to be picked up. Small, skinny children with slicked black hair went to schools that accepted public donations of sugar, rice, and cloth. The coconut water was salty, the vegetables were small and withered, and the milk was watery. This was a place you drove through with the windows up. It was easy to get swindled here, even if you had lived here all your life.

This was a town where monkeys carried away abandoned puppies and birds flew straight into homes. Thunderclouds circled the skies but never brought any rain. This was a town where penny frogs abounded all year round. They were supposed to only come out during the monsoons, but here, Thamarai found them all the time, smeared into the road or baked by the scorching sun into tiny hard corpses. You could not help stepping on the live ones or riding over them with your cycle. Thamarai used to catch them and cup them in her hands, looking at their dark eyes and tiny feet. Once she had picked one up to show off at school and the girls had backed away from her in utter disgust. Thamarai stopped picking up frogs after that.

She had also seen small turtles emerge during the monsoons, even though turtles were not supposed to live in this region at all. Near her house, a dust devil would snap up and swirl every day, in the exact same place, during the summer. Fireflies would appear in the same tree every night. There was the woman at the shop who was friendly and chatty, but whom no one else had ever seen. Thamarai soon became used to all of it. Birds flew, the sun set, and people lived and died. If something happened, it happened. There was no other way to look at it.

***

Two years later, Thamarai was still living in the same town. She had become more like the other girls now; she had lost weight, and stooped when she walked. She had done badly in her 9th exams and slightly better in her 10th. Strange happenings continued to haunt her, the most notable being a disembodied voice she kept hearing in the bathroom in the early mornings. She had also found the carcass of something in the backyard which looked exactly like a tiny dragon. As always, she tried to take these things in stride. She would not talk to the voice in the bathroom, but she did keep the tiny dragon carcass.

One morning, during the first week of 11th standard, Thamarai cycled to maths tuition, savouring the crisp air. She could smell woodsmoke, incense, and the acridness of burning plastic. Gravel crunched and popped under her tires.

The world looked so sharp and gorgeous that she could feel it slice through her every time she moved. Something hurt, but that same something was also filling her with an anticipation of painfully bright possibilities. She had seen it in the small, dirty window above the sink, in the dapples of sunlight sliding over and under the dark green leaves of a mango tree, and in the unripe mangoes that hid in its shadows. She had scalded her tongue on her morning cup of Horlicks and still, everything shimmered and winked.

Maybe someone was going to die today. Or something terrible was going to happen to her. Or maybe she was going to get her period. Unbearably beautiful mornings sometimes happened when she was going to get her period.

As always, the road was littered with the remains of a violent night. Thamarai had cycled this road to maths tuition almost every day for two years, and every morning it looked as though something catastrophic had occurred. Dead rats, scorpions, snakes, and frogs dotted the gravel, always in multiple pieces, some of them partially smudged into the road. Today there was an animal Thamarai couldn't recognize: its face was spread against the rust-coloured ground, its mouth crushed open, with one eye smeared across the dirt. Nearby were some used sanitary napkins that had been pulled out of garbage bags by the street dogs and ripped into small clouds of cotton flecked with dark blood.

It was a terrible road, a series of sudden ditches broken by jagged stones. It was especially treacherous during the monsoons, when snakes swam languidly in the deep potholes, pedestrians stumbled and fell, and careful cyclists slowly tipped over into the swift, brown water. Every few years the panchayat would try to tar the road, but the gravel would soon chew through the surface until it was patchy and pitted once again.

The sides of the road were strewn with empty McDowell's whisky tetra packs and quarter-bottles of Old Monk rum. Thamarai imagined young men in lungis and combed-back hair crowding onto the road every night, quietly getting drunk and rubbing their faces against the stiff bras of old prostitutes who held them like mothers. She had once seen a few minutes of a blue film in which an older woman had seduced a young man by showing him her bra, which looked like it was made of sheet metal. The man had laid his head on the woman's chest in such a slow, sad manner that Thamarai was sure he was going to burst into tears.

At the end of the road, an open manhole lay yawning up at the sky. Open manholes lay all over the nagar, a testament to the time when the panchayat had tried to build some kind of neighbourhood sewage system but abandoned the project because there was nowhere for the sewage to go.

Thamarai turned onto a narrower but equally terrible road. Then she came to a stop in front of a small house that looked like a cube.

Thamarai did not like maths tuition. She did not like maths, and she didn't like the fact that she had to learn it in two places. Also, she did not like to think about what had happened with the old woman.

Despite this, Thamarai made it a point to attend every single class, including the Saturday revision tests that nobody else ever came for, not even the tuition master's own daughter, S.T. Priya. On those Saturday afternoons, Thamarai would arrive early and wrench the tuition master out of his siesta. He would then scribble a few questions on the nearest piece of scrap paper and stare dully into space while Thamarai sincerely attempted to answer them. She never answered anything correctly because she never knew what she was doing. Mathematics to her was a mishmash of symbols, numbers, and formulae that she remembered seeing in various textbooks. Her answers were driven more by feeling than anything else, and were always written in blocks of straight lines, like a poem. But the tuition master didn't care. At the end of the test, without even looking at her answers, he would take her notebook and work out the sums neatly for her.

"You just have to mug up," he would say. "There's no other way. Students like you have to mug."

Thamarai would beam and nod. She never managed to mug anything up, but she wanted the tuition master to be happy.

On that particular morning, she sat in her usual place at the table, looking up at the unhealthy trees. She avoided looking at the house and focused instead on the sky. It was unnaturally blue and seemed far too close. She felt that if she raised her arm high enough, she would catch it on her fingertips.

She reached up and slowly turned her hand, as though she was scooping out a part of the sky.

"What are you doing?" asked S.T. Priya suspiciously. She had plopped herself down in one of the chairs and already looked bored with the day.

"Everything looks so bright today," Thamarai said. "No?"

S.T. Priya frowned and looked around. "Looks like it always does," she said.

"See the sky though. See that blue. Isn't the blue very blue today?"

"Loose-u," S.T. Priya muttered to herself, opening her notebook.

"You look nice today, too," said Thamarai. It was true; S.T. Priya was glowing. The richness of her dark brown skin was contrasting beautifully with her large, bright eyes. Maybe she always looked like that, and Thamarai had only noticed today.

S.T. Priya looked at her narrowly. "Don't put ice," she said.

"No ice. Really I'm saying. You're a nice-looking girl. Even though you're dark."

"Oh, thanks very much," said S.T. Priya sarcastically.

"I'm seriously saying pa, you're—"

"Dei, don't irritate in the morning!"

S.T. Priya got up and disappeared into the house again. Thamarai sighed; she knew she shouldn't have said anything. S.T. Priya did not know what to do when someone complimented her. Her usual reaction was to assume that she was being mocked, which was why she had become sullen. Now she would unnecessarily snap at Thamarai for the next few days. Thamarai would not apologize—because why should she apologize?—and S.T. Priya would get even angrier because Thamarai was not apologizing. This was the general timbre of their relationship. The girls did not like each other, but they acted as if they were close friends. They had tried smoking together; they had tried summoning ghosts together; and they took all the same tuitions and classes. They sat together on the second last bench in school. S.T. Priya had a habit of moving her knees from side to side while sitting, and Thamarai had picked up the habit of moving her own legs too, like an echo. They were used to each other, and that familiarity was often mistaken for friendship.

S.T. Priya was scared of her tuition-master father but had an indifferent attitude towards most other things. Her mother kept an impressive collection of Tamil movie songbooks stacked neatly under the family's single bed. S.T. Priya brought these to school, and when others were studying or chatting, she would sing entire songbooks for the entertainment of whoever was nearby—usually Thamarai.

"Oh lord!" S.T. Priya had crooned one afternoon. These lyrics were in English and she always felt the best way to sing English words was to drag them out with great feeling."Please answer my prayer!"

She was not a good singer, and when she was not very familiar with a song, she would simply make up her own tune.

"What movie?" Thamarai had asked.

"*Gnana Oli.*"

"It's not nice."

"Yenna not nice?"

"Your singing."

"Did I ask you?"

"I'm just saying."

"Who wants you to say anything. Shall I sing it again?"

"Yes."

S.T. Priya also had an undying love for the actress Bhanupriya, who she viewed as proof that a woman could be beautiful and successful, even if she was dark. She had a small collection of Bhanupriya's pictures, all cut from the newspaper, which she safely kept in the back of her rough notebook. She was careful to keep them away from her younger sister, who was constantly trying to get her hands on them so she could tear them up. Thamarai had once made the mistake of saying that S.T. Priya looked a lot like Bhanupriya, which was true. S.T. Priya had gotten so upset that she wouldn't talk to Thamarai for a week. S.T. Priya thought of herself as being *too* dark, her teeth too big, her hair too unruly, and her overall self being just too ugly to look even remotely like Bhanupriya.

S.T. Priya's favourite place in the world was her grandmother's house in town. She went there as often as she could and was forever telling Thamarai how amazing it was. The house was always cool, she said. Better than having A/C. Her grandmother loved to see her and, no matter the season, there would be salted, soft-boiled peanuts waiting for her, freshly harvested with the scent of the soil still on them. Thamarai had once asked if she could come along, but S.T. Priya had said no.

S.T. Priya did not like girls with short hair. She didn't like girls who wore midis all the time. And she *really* didn't like girls who wore t-shirts, especially if they didn't wear a chemise underneath. This dislike could be traced to one birthday a few years ago, when S.T. Priya herself had the audacity to wear a t-shirt to school as her birthday coloured dress. She had worn a thick and bulky petticoat underneath, and a dupatta over it; the outfit had nevertheless been risqué enough to induce a handful of young men to follow her home, whistling and making kissing noises. When she finally got to her house, tears were streaming fast down her face and her whole body was shaking. Her father beat her and said she wasn't allowed to wear t-shirts again. Later, he tracked down the young men who had followed her, dragged them out into the street in the middle of the night, and beat them too.

***

S.T. Priya's house had a mysterious room with a wooden door that always remained locked. The door was painted bright blue and looked startlingly uncomfortable against the grey cement walls. The landlord had initially offered the use of the room for an extra Rs. 500/- per month. The offer was declined, and the landlord had locked the door with a large padlock that had long since rusted shut. As far as the family knew, the room hadn't been opened in years, and nobody seemed to know what was inside. Perhaps broken furniture or a collection of old bureaus, they thought. Maybe the room was empty.

S.T. Priya did not like the locked room. It annoyed her, mainly because Thamarai kept telling her it was haunted.

"You should move," Thamarai once said.

"Say no more. We will start moving now itself. I mean if *you* tell us to move, how can we not listen," said S.T. Priya.

"Really? You will?"

"Loose-u, you think anyone will move just because you say so? Will anyone listen to you and your stupid mouth?"

"Oh."

"Why are you such a crack actually?"

"But that room—"

"Say one more word about the room and see what I do to you."

"Okay."

"Waste room. Stupid."

"Sorry."

The room was in fact haunted, but Thamarai was the only person who knew it. One Saturday afternoon in 10th standard, S.T. Priya's family had gone to town, leaving Thamarai alone on the veranda to do her weekly revision test. The afternoon had been very still, and Thamarai was on the point of dozing off when she noticed that the door of the room was open. A small, bony, grey woman was shuffling out, grumbling softly to herself. It sounded like the rustling of insect wings. At first, Thamarai didn't think there was anything odd about the old woman. Obviously, this was some relative who had come to stay, and they had opened the extra room for her.

"Hai paati," Thamarai shouted. Then as an afterthought she added, "Do you need any help?"

Thamarai never helped anyone with anything, but when it came to the elderly, she always made it a point to ask, just to be polite.

The old woman turned and looked at Thamarai. Her face was nothing but a mass of deep wrinkles. She had no eyes or nose, and her mouth looked like a sloppy gash across her face. Thamarai watched with growing dismay as the old woman's lower jaw began to drop until it was touching the floor. Her mouth hung open, black as tar, looking like it was about to swallow everything. A strong, wet scent of death flooded the air, and a gurgling sound seemed to be coming from her throat.

Suddenly, the old woman was standing right in front of Thamarai. The smell of death and decay was on Thamarai's tongue, suffusing her whole body.

Before Thamarai knew what was happening, the old woman had jammed a fist full of sharp, dry fingers into her mouth. Thamarai tried to pull away but she could not move. The old woman roughly dragged her by the jaw to the back of the house, singing something in a horrific, high-pitched voice. Thamarai stumbled along, simultaneously hopeful and scared that someone might see them. Branches scratched at her face. Then the old woman let go, and was standing in front of her again, slowly stretching out her arm. Thamarai could see seven fingers on the outstretched hand.

And then the old woman pounced on her.

Her bony legs were wrapped tightly around Thamarai's neck, while her hands wrenched open her mouth. The old woman's grip was like iron, and no matter how Thamarai struggled, she could not move. With growing horror, she watched as the old woman's face came closer to her, until it looked like she was going to stick her head into Thamarai's mouth. She heard a sound like a gurgle, and then something cold and slimy was running down her throat. It smelled like the entire earth was rotting inside her mouth. There were pieces of something soft on her tongue. Thamarai gagged.

Without realizing what she was doing, she ran to the nearby tap and began retching while scratching at her throat. The smell, the feeling of the soft chunks on her tongue and the cold sliminess running down her throat was overwhelming. She desperately grabbed the blue washing soap, broke a piece off with her teeth and tried to chew it. It just made her retch again, but this time, the strong scent of detergent almost overpowered the smell of rot. She eventually got a hold of herself enough to vigorously rub the soap over her teeth and tongue while holding her mouth open under the tap. The old woman had vomited in her mouth. The more she thought about it, the sicker she got. The unfairness of it hit her hard; she had done nothing, and this malevolent old woman had grabbed her like death and vomited in her mouth.

After Thamarai had been rubbing her tongue with blue soap for a while, she realized that the old woman had disappeared. With soap suds and saliva running down her chin, Thamarai slowly made her way to the front yard. The entire street seemed strangely empty. She looked inside the house and saw that the door to the mysterious room was locked again, the padlock sitting dully on the latch like it had never been opened. The old woman was nowhere to be found. Thamarai sat stunned, unable to believe what had just happened to her.

Finally she neatly folded her test paper, placed it in the centre of the table, and left before the family returned.

***

Name: Paati.
Danger Classification: Generally harmless, at least when found outside the GGHSS.
Description: Greasy grey hair tied in a bun, checked cotton sari and a yellow cloth bag. Often has diabetes. Fourteen fingers and fourteen toes. Does not consume water.
Nesting Habits: We can generally find paatis in joint family homes, where there are already so many people that an extra old lady goes unnoticed. She will not stay in one place for too long, because if her true nature is discovered, she will be trapped in that place forever. If someone keeps asking about the paati's family and where she comes from, the paati will leave early the next morning and never be seen again. Contrary to popular opinion, a paati does not steal or damage items in or around her nesting place. They are happy to accept whatever is given to them, but are incapable of taking anything on their own. They will enter family life seamlessly, and can often be found assisting with cooking, supervising the help, or watching very small children.
Social Interactions: Easily identified by her conversation, the paati usually asks very generic questions like "So then what happened with that boy?" or "Why do you look so tired now?". This gives her the appearance of being well-versed in the family gossip. Paatis are adept at creating and navigating conversation without actually contributing anything meaningful.
Special Note on Paatis of the GGHSS: Paatis trapped in the GGHSS can be identified by their faces, which will be nothing more than a mass of wrinkles. The paatis of the GGHSS have all been pulled in from outside, possibly while straying too close to the school. They quickly become decrepit and bony, their faces resembling bundles of cloth. They shuffle about the halls at night, collecting

old papers, forgotten pens, and fallen strings of dead jasmines. It is said that they move easily through walls and are very bad-tempered. It is always best to avoid the GGHSS paatis.

***

The potentially beautiful morning seemed to be dissolving as Thamarai sat alone on the veranda, listening to the tuition sir hack and cough while he brushed his teeth. She glanced at the blue door and was relieved to see it was still locked.

Then Thamarai heard the sound of a sturdy TVS moped crunching to a stop on the gravelled road. She looked up at the rider and immediately broke into a grin. Behind her, S.T. Priya came to the door, and her face, too, relaxed into a sweet, gentle smile.

"Yenna ya, late?" asked S.T. Priya.

The girl on the TVS shook her head, locked her moped, wiped sweat from her face and shook her head again. This was Prasanna. She was very flustered at the moment and as a result, she spoke in one long, rushed sentence.

"I slept off ya," said Prasanna. "I woke up at four to study then Amma came at six and sleep was just filling my eyes so Amma said okay you sleep for some time I will wake you when the water is hot for your bath so I said okay and I was just knocked out and Amma forgot to wake me I just had my milk and came."

"Take a breath," said S.T. Priya with a chuckle.

"My mind is all upside down I wanted to see those sums I don't know what I'm going to do." Prasanna gave her face one last wipe and opened her textbook.

Thamarai sat beaming at her.

"What?" asked Prasanna, looking up.

"You are looking nice today too."

"What's this?" Prasanna asked, turning to S.T. Priya.

"Who knows? She said the same to me," said S.T. Priya. "Maybe she wants someone to say it back to her."

Thamarai had been falling in love with Prasanna for almost a year. She loved the way Prasanna stooped when she walked, she loved how Prasanna carried her handkerchief, and she loved Prasanna's handwriting. Prasanna was the only person in the world who seemed concerned about Thamarai's future. She advised Thamarai about life and further studies. She got upset when Thamarai talked about jumping into wells or going missing. Sometimes Thamarai would skip her lunch, just so Prasanna would become concerned and sit close beside her, talking to her about acidity and offering to buy her Milk Bikis.

"Everything is beautiful today da," Thamarai whispered to Prasanna. "I mean, it *was* beautiful. Now it's just okay."

"What do you mean?"

"I don't know."

"Seri. Did you want to tell me anything else?"

"Not right now."

"Fine," said Prasanna, looking at her textbook. Thamarai went back to admiring the sky.

***

Thamarai wasn't sure why Prasanna came to tuition, but she was glad she did. Things were just nicer when she was there. Everyone liked her. In school, the whole class wanted her to go to college and get a job in Chennai. They wanted her to wear salwar kameez and have her own money. When Prasanna finally married, they wanted her husband to be like a Raymond's model.

In class, Prasanna sat directly in front of Thamarai. The scent of her talcum powder, soap, and sweat would often waft onto Thamarai's face in the afternoons when the sea breeze came in. When this happened, old Tamil love songs would start playing in Thamarai's head. They would keep playing till the end of the day, making her dream about what it would be like to be a man. Even though Prasanna wasn't class leader, she was often asked to stand in front of the class during morning assembly. Everyone wanted to see her, some because she was smart, some because she could speak English, and some because she was naturally light-skinned. Seeing her standing up front gave the impression that everyone in the school was like her.

Eleventh standard was the year that a number of girls in Thamarai's class became beautiful. Many of them had blossomed into striking young women, with a few even resembling popular TV actresses. Prasanna had reached movie star level; she looked like Meena, Revathi, and Jyothika all mixed together. She had caramel-coloured eyes and a spray of acne on each of her cheeks. When she wore coloured dress on Saturdays, she looked like a successful, worried, modern girl.

Prasanna was also a genuinely good person. She did not know how to be malicious or how to see it in others. She was hard-working, generous, destined for great things. She was everything that Thamarai wasn't.

Prasanna had lived in this town all her life. Her family occupied quarters on campus at the local college. She enjoyed the benefits that came with being an orthodox Brahmin and the daughter of a college lecturer in a conservative Hindu town. The town was casteist in the way so many small towns were. Lower castes did not enter the upper caste houses where they worked; instead they washed dishes and clothes by the outside tap. It was a town that applauded mixed-caste marriages in the movies and looked down on them in real life.

***

In general, the day always got worse for Thamarai after maths tuition. Even today, which had started off with such possibility, was devolving into just another day. Thamarai felt ridiculous for having thought it would be different from any other.

After maths tuition, the three girls lingered near S.T. Priya's front gate, chatting about nothing in particular, readying themselves to head to physics tuition. Prasanna got on her TVS 50 and S.T. Priya got on her old Luna moped. Thamarai put her books into her bag and snapped it onto the carrier of her cycle. At the very bottom of her bag, she caught a glimpse of the botany record notebook, its tatters poking out as if trying to catch some wayward sunlight. *I should really throw that out,* she thought to herself. It was odd how she kept forgetting,

"Seri," said Prasanna, touching Thamarai gently on the shoulder. As always, Thamarai felt something surge inside her. She wished they didn't have to go to physics tuition. She wished the sky would split and pour forth an avalanche of December flowers that would drown S.T. Priya. She wished that Prasanna would then take her home for a breakfast of soft idlies and podi.

But none of these things happened. Prasanna and S.T. Priya were soon sputtering out of sight, and Thamarai was left to doggedly cycle behind them alone.

This was when Thamarai always started to feel sorry for herself. She was the only one among the tuition-going girls who did not have a TVS or a Luna. Instead, she was stuck with a second-hand, rusty, dark green Hercules bicycle that kept trying to eat the hem of her skirt. Whenever a tuition class ended, the other girls would smoothly and swiftly disperse on their mopeds, laughing amongst themselves, not even breaking a sweat. No one waited for Thamarai. No one said they would ride slowly, so she could keep pace with them. Even Prasanna always rode off, leaving Thamarai trying to catch up with her, and failing.

The more Thamarai thought about all this, the more unfair it seemed, and the sorrier she felt for herself. It was at times like these, when there was no one else around, that something inexplicable would happen. Today, it was a handful of dragonflies that accompanied her all the way to physics tuition. They sat on her shoulders and arms and crawled slowly across the back of her hand while she tried not to panic. When she finally arrived at physics tuition a little late, covered in sweat and dust, the dragonflies swiftly flew off into the distance.

Upstairs, the other girls were fresh and silent, watching her as she came in and took her seat. Thamarai had a sticky lump of jealousy and self-pity in her throat, so concentrated that it made it difficult to speak.

Physics tuition was held in the home of a girl Thamarai did not know very well. This girl went to the local convent school and was one of the wealthier students, living in a small flat that tried its best to look like an upper-middle-class home from the movies. The flat had a dining table covered with a plastic tablecloth. The living area had plastic chairs, a wooden two-seater, and a TV in the corner, covered by a flowered plastic sheet. A cricket bat, chunky white sneakers, *Tinkle* comics, various caps, and *Competition Success* magazines showed how much the son of the house was cherished. Cheap plastic items jostled against each other inside the showcase, including souvenirs from Nigeria and Yugoslavia. The showcase also housed a large lizard that pooped on everything.

Thamarai had no idea what was happening in physics tuition either. But unlike the maths tuition master, the physics tuition master, Gopalan Sir, was very focused on making Thamarai pass with flying colours. Thin to the point of being scrawny, with unnerving bright eyes, Gopalan Sir had shocking tufts of white hair growing out of each ear and a tendency to throw his arms about when speaking. Despite being elderly, he always had a lot of energy, and this was frankly frightening to behold.

The most interesting thing about Gopalan Sir was that he wore incredibly ill-fitting dentures. Whenever he spoke, they slipped and skidded all over his mouth, constantly threatening to launch into the air and hit someone in the eye. Like most things in his life, he had got them free from an old student. His old students also gave him free air for his cycle and free cloth for his trousers. Gopalan Sir claimed he had never paid for a train or bus ticket, and he was particularly fond of boasting about the rice, legumes, bananas, peanuts, and mangoes he got for free. Even his dentures had been absolutely free. His version of the story was that a student, who was now a big dentist in Chennai, had come to Gopalan Sir's home to pay his respects. He had come in a white Maruti 800 car, wearing socks and shoes. During their conversation, Gopalan Sir had simply mentioned in passing that his teeth were giving him problems. The old student immediately insisted on giving him dentures, free of charge.

The other version of this story, the one everyone else told, was quite different. The dentures had not been given for free, only *taken* for free. Gopalan Sir was notorious for cornering old students and hinting at things he needed; the student would wearily agree to provide it for a discount, and Gopalan Sir would take it for free. The student would repeatedly follow up for payment and Gopalan Sir would repeatedly not pay. At some point the student would simply give up. With the former student who had made the dentures, there had been no white Maruti, socks, or shoes. This particular student had no trustworthy dental qualifications at all. He had purchased his degree, and was now pretending to be a dentist in a clinic called Swetee Smile that was hidden in a small, crowded lane somewhere on the outskirts of Chennai. There was a good chance that when making Gopalan Sir's dentures, the former student had made them carelessly, knowing he would not be paid for them. Which was why, while Gopalan Sir spoke passionately about kinetic energy, his dentures danced around his mouth and Thamarai sat mesmerized by them. Once he had actually spat them out entirely, and Thamarai was always grateful that she had been there to witness the event.

Thamarai had to sit next to Gopalan Sir during class because he had often caught her daydreaming or on the verge of falling asleep. He was on a mission to make her learn, and he believed that having her sit next to him was somehow conducive to making this happen. From this vantage point, Thamarai sat quietly and didn't pay attention. She no longer knew what "paying attention" meant. She tried understanding whatever notes he jotted down during class. She tried listening to what he was saying. She frowned at her textbook, then her notebook, then her textbook again in an excellent imitation of a studious person. But nothing seemed to work, and she couldn't think of what else "pay attention" might mean.

"And you ma? What are you going to give me when you become a successful doctor?" Gopalan Sir asked Thamarai. She gasped like she had been slapped.

"Aiyyo, no sir," she said quietly.

"Engineer then."

"Sir!" she said, her voice trembling a little in shock. The fact that he was even suggesting these things unnerved her.

"Then what are you going to be?"

"IAS," said S.T. Priya. "She will join the Indian Adupaangarai Service, sir,"

The other girls giggled, except Prasanna, who looked at Thamarai with a touch of pity.

"Sir she's not interested in anything, sir," said Prasanna.

"So what? Interest is not necessary ma. You don't need interest to do well in exams. And you WILL do well," said Gopalan Sir, flinging his arm out like he didn't want it anymore. "Even if I lose my life in the process!"

"Please don't die because of me sir," Thamarai said, on the verge of tears now. "Even I wouldn't die for me."

"You are not so dull as you think. See, you have understood

this, no? Isn't it?" he said, pointing to a number of diagrams and formulae.

"Sir?"

"I said you have understood this."

"I have?"

"Have you or haven't you."

"Sir—"

"Because if you have understood this, then you have understood this also, isn't it."

"Sir?"

"Isn't it? Then what is the problem?"

"But I can't understand anything," she blurted out.

Gopalan Sir took a beat, like he was calming himself.

"How can you not understand this?"

"I can't understand anything sir. Anything. When I ask people my doubts they think I am trying to be funny. Everyone mistakes me. I can't understand anything and no one will help me," said Thamarai, on the verge of tears again. The idea of someone seeking knowledge and not getting any help moved her deeply.

"Okay. What exactly do you not understand. Tell me. I will say."

Thamarai took a deep breath and looked at the paper with the various notes he had written down.

"See this sir," said Thamarai, pointing to a formula.

$$\frac{\varepsilon}{\varepsilon_0} = \varepsilon_r$$

"Dielectric constant of the medium! Of the—?" he said, waiting for Thamarai to finish the sentence.

"But why is it like that?"

"Like what?"

"Why is there a backwards 3?"

"That is not 3! 3 is like this. 3."

"Then what is it?"

"That is dielectric constant of the medium."

"The whole thing is? Or just the backwards 3?"

"My father said that is epsilon, some Greek alphabet," said Prasanna.

"But why is it that?"

"What kind of question is this ma?" said Gopalan Sir, throwing his arms about.

"Did someone make this up?"

"People who have more knowledge than you discovered it. Enough?"

"But why?"

"Why what?"

"Why dielectric constant of the medium? Why is it that?"

Gopalan Sir was silent. Thamarai had never seen him still and quiet before, and it was unsettling. For some reason, it felt like he was dead. Then Gopalan Sir pointedly turned away from her and started teaching the others. He ignored her for the rest of the class, and did not say anything when she mumbled "Thank you sir" before leaving.

Downstairs, the girls applauded her for the entertainment during physics tuition. Even S.T. Priya kept laughing and saying, "Super! Super!" Thamarai brightened at this feeling of being a daredevil among them, until she noticed that Prasanna looked visibly upset and wouldn't laugh at any of her jokes.

"Go and apologize to Sir," Prasanna said to her.

"For what?"

"Go!"

"What did I do?"

Prasanna would not look at her, and Thamarai panicked. She must have done something terrible without even knowing it. Prasanna might never speak to her again. Thamarai raced back up to the flat, where Gopalan Sir was having a tumbler of coffee before heading to his next tuition. He had made himself thoroughly comfortable, as if he was in his own house.

"Sir, sorry sir," said Thamarai. The aroma of the fresh filter coffee wafted towards her and her mouth watered. It was the good kind of filter coffee. Not too sweet, not too bitter, not too much milk; it smelled rich, warm, and nourishing.

"Why are you saying sorry now?" he asked.

"Sir..."

"Did your friends tell you to?"

"Yes sir."

He drank his coffee slowly and noisily. Thamarai watched him intently.

"Can I have some coffee, sir?" Thamarai asked. Students never asked for coffee, but Thamarai sometimes did stupid things. Gopalan Sir looked at her, then called out to the kitchen for another cup. A small girl brought it out and handed it to Thamarai with surprise. Thamarai drank it slowly, letting the flavour spill all over her tongue. It was very, very good.

"Seri," said Gopalan Sir. "You finish your coffee."

He got up and left. Thamarai listened to the sounds in the kitchen and realized that no one in the house knew she was still there. She worried that some male member of the family would come out shirtless and she would have to see his nipples. She kept her empty cup on the table and quietly left. By the time she got back to her cycle, the rest of the girls were already in the distance, on their way to chemistry tuition, the third and final tuition before school. A warm and comfortable sense of jealousy settled inside her again. Jealousy gave her terrible acidity and bad breath, but it also gave her a sense of belonging. It was in her moments of jealousy that she saw quite clearly that she did not belong anywhere, and this in itself was very comforting.

The girls had completely disappeared by now, and Thamarai's jealousy wrapped itself, comfortably, around her heart. She remembered the coffee and decided she would tell the others about it. The girls would say things like, "That crazy Thamarai. You should have seen how she spoke in physics tuition! And then? She got a coffee! She just asked and he gave her! None of us got coffee." Thamarai thought about this at length and ended up being so late for chemistry tuition that she decided to skip it and went straight to school instead.

***

The GGHSS or Government Girls Higher Secondary School was nestled between a set of railroad tracks and a large open drain. In contrast to the town, the school was oddly unremarkable, almost bland. It consisted of a main building and a number of smaller sheds which seemed to have been tossed around at random. There was a cycle stand, a stretch of sandy ground that extended from the Noon Meal Scheme outdoor kitchen to the front gate. There was also a broken basketball court and a hand pump for water. The main building had a ground floor and first floor; on the ground floor was the Headmistress's office, which was a very dark room well suited for afternoon naps. It looked like any other government school. It was too ordinary.

The school offered both Tamil and English medium classes; there was only one English medium class per standard. 9th and 11th standard were considered somewhat useless; no one took them as seriously as the more important 10th and 12th standards. This was reflected in the seating arrangements. The 6th to 9th standard girls sat on the floor, with some of the 6th standard classes sitting outdoors. The 10th and 12th standard classes got benches and tables that sat three to a bench. The 11th standard had benches for the lucky ones and the floor for everyone else.

Since 11th standard didn't really matter, almost all classes were free periods. The few students who studied used that time to prepare for their 12th exams. Some girls hadn't even bothered to buy the 11th standard texts, opting instead to dive head-first into next year's syllabus. 11A was the English medium class, and consisted of different types of academics. There were the first-row girls, who studied so excessively and with such fervour that they always gave themselves diarrhoea. There were those who did not study in class, opting instead to cram at home at the last minute and get average marks; these were usually the daughters of professors from the local college, whose seats for their bachelor's degree were already assured. There were the girls who studied half-heartedly, did badly, and didn't care, because they were just going to get married once school was finished. There were the girls who studied doggedly and did badly. And there were the girls who did not study at all, using the endless number of free periods to pick lice, draw kolams in their notebooks, play the bangle game, and chat.

Thamarai fell at the meeting place of all these groups, sitting precisely at the point where one didn't study at all and didn't do anything else either. She was famous for simply sitting there, staring straight ahead and barely moving. This is how she spent most of her time in class. She would sometimes watch what was happening around her, or watch her thoughts, as if she was asleep but still aware of what was going on.

At lunch time, S.T. Priya would lug Thamarai and Prasanna to the corridor to eat lunch. Thamarai always had the same thing—old rice, curd, fried snake gourd and a touch of pickle. Her mouth watered when she saw the other girls' food. S.T. Priya would rarely share, believing it was better to exchange lunches than to share them. She had no love at all for old rice and fried snake gourd, though. Prasanna, on the other hand, was more than happy to share. Sometimes she brought fried potato, chapathis, bitter gourd, or tamarind rice. On one occasion, Prasanna had brought Maggi noodles; Thamarai had eaten them all, not sharing any with S.T. Priya, who ended up taking it very badly. It wasn't that Thamarai loved to eat; she was simply hungry all the time. Prasanna had once asked if Thamarai had tapeworms. Thamarai thought she probably did, because it seemed like no matter what she ate, she was always hungry afterwards.

After lunch, an absolutely magical band of sunlight would settle inside the 11A classroom and stay until school was over. During times like this, Thamarai completely forgot about all the inexplicable things—the children with hands for heads, the unseasonable frogs and turtles, the paati.

As the afternoon progressed, the sunlight would grow richer and mellower, giving everything and everyone it touched a beauty that could never be seen anywhere else. This was when Thamarai ended up falling in love with some girl, simply because she looked beautiful in that afternoon sunlight.

The rest of the school day would either be relaxed or filled with an electric energy. On a relaxed afternoon, girls would lay their heads on their school bags, talking to each other in hushed tones. Some girls would fall asleep. On an electric afternoon, a restlessness ran through them, and someone would inevitably ask Prasanna to sing movie songs while Thamarai banged out a rhythm on the top of a desk. The magic of these afternoons was unforgettable. An ordinary movie song became something that the girls would remember many years later, with an overwhelming feeling of nostalgia. Each girl would smile and sing along, forming a circle where everyone touched and leaned against each other—class enmities set aside so that, for that afternoon, everyone was a friend.

Once the last bell rang, Thamarai gathered her bag, took out her cycle key and headed down to the cycle stand. Before the girls had got their mopeds, Thamarai would cycle home with Prasanna and S.T. Priya on either side of her, the latter always swerving dangerously towards her so Thamarai was in constant fear of being knocked down. They would quietly chat with each other, keeping their eyes low and on the road. At one point, the three of them would break off to take different routes. Prasanna would turn into the college lecturer's quarters, S.T. Priya would continue down the street, and Thamarai would turn and cycle down the terrible road to her home. The world would look magnificent. The scrub brush in the empty fields, the large rocks, the reddish dirt, everything seemed to hold a glow that made Thamarai feel like her heart was going to break. By the time she was finally home, the sun would be lower in the sky and the glow would be gone. The world would be dim, like a smudged drawing. Later, when the moon came out, everything would look like it was lit by a single white tubelight.

***

Name: The Sand Worms of Patriotism.
Danger Classification: Harmless but extremely moody and unpredictable, given to sudden bursts of wild energy during which they toss 6th standard girls up in the air at random.
Description: Gigantic fossorial worms with large, ungainly pale yellow bodies. Their eyes are quite small and rise up on thin, red stalks. The inside of the mouth is a spiral staircase which leads down either into the worm's stomach or to some desolate plain of supernatural mystery that we have not had the chance to explore.
General Behaviour: Though their actions are usually erratic, there is one activity the sand worms indulge in regularly. When the national flag is raised and unfurled, and the bougainvillea flowers wrapped therein are starting to drop like dead weights to the ground, the sand worms will rise to the surface and fling themselves bodily into the air. As they have a tendency to throw themselves up and out, they often splatter against nearby buildings, though this does not kill them. These sand worms also have an intimidating sense of patriotism. In fact, it is

physically impossible to deny their patriotism. Those who have tried have ended up with shredded tongues or recurring bouts of clinical depression. These sand worms have the very blood of India running through their veins, blood the colour of the tricolour, blood that smells like sandalwood and Khadi stores.

In terms of diet, these worms enjoy eating large mouthfuls of sand. They tend to chew slowly and enjoy listening to the sound of the grains being ground to a fine powder by the stairs inside their mouths.

Social Interactions: Sand worms do not like swallowing girls. In fact, they hate girls intensely and are one of the few supernatural entities known to be vocal men's rights activists. They are also the founding species of the well-known paranormal group "Just Because We Hate Girls Doesn't Mean We Are Gay". Despite this, they will always swallow at least two girls each time they fling themselves up and out. These girls land on the staircase and immediately begin walking down in a highly excited manner, much to the disappointment of the worm. The girls are never seen again but are always reported to look happy and hopeful as they descend into the supernatural depths of the sand worm.

***

Thamarai lived next door to an antisocial family of four. There were two elderly parents and a pair of sisters who appeared to be in their thirties. Thamarai had made the mistake of being friendly when she had first moved in, and from then on, the sisters had never let her go. They did not speak to anyone except Thamarai. Their house looked like a small, dirty box that had been abandoned in the middle of a yard, which was overgrown with brush and small, tangled trees. The windows were never opened due to the constant threat of mosquitoes and young men peeking in. The sisters themselves hardly came out at all, except during the evenings, when the two of them would walk briskly to and fro on the terrace. Once a week the floors of the house were cleaned with a thick bar of blue soap. Mosquito coils were lit every evening and suffocated any insect that was unfortunate enough to be caught indoors. Lizards were chased relentlessly, with one sister sweeping them off the wall with a grass broom, and the other beating them to death with a coconut broom. They ate the same vegetables every day: drumstick, monkey beans, chayote squash, and a watery spinach gravy, with all the vegetables somehow managing to taste the same.

The high point of the sisters' lives was when they had attended the GGHSS. During that time, they cycled to school, had friends, and spent a short time every day outside in the fresh air. Their favourite pastime had been to gossip maliciously about their classmates and teachers and then to share this gossip with their parents when they got home. After failing their 12th standard exams, the sisters were kept at home, waiting to be married off. Years later, they were still unmarried and sitting at home, like so many other akkas from the GGHSS. Every morning they cooked the day's food and tidied up the house. Then the afternoon would be spent rewatching 80s Tamil action movies on a VHS player, their most precious possession. In the evenings, they would have a cup of tea, take their daily brisk walk, and then watch Doordarshan programming until ten p.m.

They wore stiff cotton nighties with thick cotton dupattas pinned to their shoulders. Their hair was always well oiled and braided, with a single strand of jasmine pinned right above the braid. They each had one toe that was abnormally shorter than the rest and they both had irregular periods. There was a rumour that one of them had a hole in her heart, and that once she died, the other sister would die soon after because there would be nothing for her to live for.

When Thamarai was unfortunate enough to be caught outside during the evenings, the sisters would descend on her like a couple of crows, making fun of her hair, her face, her bony body, and her existence in general. They would hungrily clamour around her for news from the school and town. Sometimes, they would ask after certain teachers, even though it had been many years since the sisters had been in school, and most of their teachers had left.

"Okay, tell what's happening," said the sisters one evening. Thamarai had tried to sneak past them, but their eyes were sharp and they easily spotted her from the terrace.

"I have maths tuition," lied Thamarai.

"Maths tuition is in the morning, don't try that with us," they said. "Now quickly, what's happening in school. What is your English Sir up to?"

The sisters were always happy to hear stories about the English Sir and how many young girls had gone to the "wrong side" because of him. Such stories implied that the sisters were on the right side, which seemed to balance out their otherwise uneventful lives.

"Come home," said the sisters. "We can speak freely."

Thamarai did not like going into the sisters' home. She did not like how they grabbed her forearm when they talked, and she didn't like their mother, who didn't like Thamarai either. What if they forced her to come inside? The thought of sitting in that suffocating house, lit only by a single lightbulb, drinking warm, hard water and eating stale biscuits that smelled like naphthalene was too much for Thamarai.

"Nono it's fine akkas. Nothing happening anyway," said Thamarai. "Usual."

"We heard your English Sir has already caught someone in your class. Who is it?"

"Appadiya?"

"Yenna appadiya. Don't play. Who is it? What is he making her do?"

It occurred to Thamarai that the only way to successfully navigate this was to make something up.

"You remember the ayah-ma? The one with the elephant's foot?" said Thamarai.

"Ayah-ma-va?! Who wants to hear about the ayah-ma?"

"That's what I was saying."

"What were you saying?"

"Illa, I mean, did you know some girls put rabbit's blood in their hair? So it will become black? And did you know there is a Draupadi temple here?"

"Have you gone insane?"

"Illa, what I meant to say was... you know what happened to that akka, right?"

"Tell, tell, which akka?"

Thamarai paused thoughtfully.

"Um... Thenmozhi? Mary? Thenmozhi Mary," she said.

"Thenmozhi Mary-va?"

"Yes."

"Who is that?"

"Anyway," said Thamarai.

"What anyway?"

"I can't think of anything else to say."

The sisters were silent. Thamarai could see herself just like these two in a few years, and it upset her greatly. But what else could the future hold? What could the future hold for girls who were simply there, for no good reason at all?

"If you are going to be so arrogant then we will leave," said the sisters icily.

"Okay then," said Thamarai. She quickly pushed her cycle onto the veranda of her house. Then she went inside. As always, it was dark, cool, and empty. Her aunt had left small, covered pots containing rice, curd, and a fried gourd in the kitchen for Thamarai's dinner. Thamarai sat on a plastic chair and sighed. She should be taking a bath; the lights needed to be turned on; the windows had to be closed so mosquitoes couldn't get in. Dinner had to be finished and everything washed up by the time her aunt arrived at ten p.m. But Thamarai did not feel like moving. She thought of the sisters. She could hear them next door, still walking on their terrace. The next time they pressed her, she would make up something better. Maybe something about a girl and a boy who had met during tuition and were planning to run away together. Thamarai always thought the sisters looked like small, sick birds when she told them stories like that. It occurred to her that she could go over and tell them now. They would be happy for days and days. She thought of this deeply and did not move, not even when it became so dark that the cockroaches came out, thinking there was no one around.

***

The 11A classroom was on the ground floor of the main school building. When Thamarai entered that morning, girls were chatting amongst themselves while adjusting their half-saris and the fresh popcorn-like jasmines in their hair. Thamarai made her way to the back where S.T. Priya was sitting, carefully re-braiding her hair.

"Did you hear about Lakshmi akka?" said S.T. Priya, not looking up from her braid.

"Which Lakshmi akka?"

"That one that went around with English Sir."

"Chee, don't say that, she's nice."

"Yenna nice. Do nice girls get caught by the English Sir? Now listen. Lakshmi akka was going to tailoring class when one black Scorpio drove up. And?"

"I don't care."

"They just grabbed her and took her around the four streets, doing god knows what. True story."

"Who is they?"

"What?"

"Who took her around?"

"Why are you asking me that?"

"Nothing like that happened."

"That's all you know, I guess. Did you know she's missing?"

"Missing ah? Then?"

"Am I telling you a bedtime story? 'Then' it seems."

In general, it was easy to make up stories about akkas because older girls went missing all the time. Families often decided that their daughters had studied enough and sent them to their native villages to stay with grandmothers or periammas. Other akkas were married off. There were akkas who stayed at home and constantly prayed for a husband and were constantly disappointed. Some went to the temple twice a day and tried to grow flowers that were completely unsuited for the local salty, clay-like soil. Others became obsessed with making "special dishes" that involved combining things like ladies' fingers with bananas and rose milk. And, of course, there were the akkas that did absolutely nothing except wear nighties with dupattas, read *Kalki* or *Kumudam* all day, and get piles.

"Hey, I'm telling you seriously," said S.T. Priya. "About Lakshmi akka."

"Seri seri."

"If you don't believe me, I don't care anyway," said S.T. Priya as she walked away.

Thamarai followed her and the other girls as they all made

their way down to morning assembly.

The assembly ground was a patch of hot dirty sand that was continually baking under a relentless sun. The 11A girls formed two indifferent lines, with the class leader P. Yamuna ensuring that everyone was silent and the lines were straight. That morning, Thamarai watched in surprise as P. Yamuna came straight up to her, grabbed her upper arm, and gently shoved her into line.

"Hey, what's all this," Thamarai said. "You don't have to touch me all over, you know."

"Ya, why unnecessarily touching," S.T. Priya chimed in. "If you ever try touching me like that I—"

"Who would ever want to touch you?" P. Yamuna said, already walking away.

"Let her just try it," S.T. Priya muttered, rolling a large louse between her thumbnails.

The PT teachers began circling the girls, whacking some small child every so often with a wooden ruler. The little, malnourished 6th standard girls looked deathly afraid and tried their best to stand perfectly still, their oversized hand-me-down uniforms hanging awkwardly off their bony shoulders. Almost everyone else was moving in some small way—switching feet in the hot sand, wiping their faces and upper arms with handkerchiefs that were already soaked with sweat. Facing the girls while comfortably ensconced in chairs on the cool, covered veranda were a couple of teachers and the headmistress, who was already asleep. Sitting next to her, staring at the 10th standard girls like he was going to eat them, was the English Sir. He was an unimpeachably respectable, utterly lecherous man, more powerful than the headmistress, a man who had gotten away with his unique brand of sexual harassment in the school for years.

Thamarai did what she could to combat the English Sir menace by staring at him in a stern and knowing manner. At least, that is what she thought she was doing. Whenever he stared at the girls, she would stare at him, hoping this would unnerve him. She thought this was important; though there was nothing that could be done about his behaviour, she wanted him to know that she was watching him, and that she knew what he was doing. But this made no impression at all on the English Sir. He never noticed that she was staring at him. Frankly, he did not really know who she was.

"SCHOOL ATTENTION," shouted the school leader from the veranda. "SCHOOL RIGHT TURN."

The entire assembly turned to the right, except for a handful of the smaller girls who turned to the left.

"Uruthi mozhi! Inthia yen thai naadu!"

The entire assembly of girls, barring Thamarai and the English Sir, repeated after the school leader dutifully. First the Thamizh Thai Vaazhthu, then the national anthem. Then two 10th standard girls sang a song about health and patriotism that annoyed Thamarai greatly. The girls were standing very seriously, keeping time by gently clapping. It occurred to her that these two had probably practiced for this. They had probably come to school early, sat under one of the trees and sang this song, again and again, like it was important.

Assembly progressed and the heat drove the lice to the top of everyone's oiled head. Thamarai hoped that something would happen; maybe someone would spot a snake. Maybe a bull would run amok among them, tossing up girls like rubber bands. Perhaps a gang of black pigs would plough through them, biting everyone in the neck. But the only thing that happened was the flag would not unfurl properly when it was raised. It was left at half-mast in a lopsided lump. That, and a line of 6th standard girls suddenly fell down, as if they had been knocked over. Thamarai saw something cutting through the sand, moving swiftly, but it disappeared before she could get a proper look at it.

***

Prasanna was standing near the front of the line. Thamarai walked up to her and put her arm around her shoulders. She rarely had the guts to do this, except on charmed afternoons when the sun covered everything and everyone was singing old movie songs. Prasanna smiled warmly at her but continued chatting with another girl. Thamarai stood there, holding Prasanna about the shoulders like she owned her. When they started walking back to the classroom, Thamarai kept her arm where it was.

"Did you say sorry?" asked Prasanna. "You did, right?"

"Ya ya."

"And did you eat in the morning?"

Prasanna asked everyone this, but Thamarai liked to pretend that she only asked her.

"Did you?" asked Prasanna.

"I can't remember. Did I?"

"Kirukki," Prasanna said with a soft smile. Thamarai's heart expanded until she could feel it inside her fingers, pulsing softly.

"You were missing from chemistry tuition," Prasanna said, with a small frown.

"I was?"

"Don't try and be funny, why didn't you come?"

"It was not an auspicious time for chemistry tuition," said Thamarai. Without realizing it, she began walking faster, and Prasanna stumbled a bit, trying to keep pace. It looked like Thamarai was dragging her along in a stubborn headlock.

"Aiyyo, my head will come off now," said Prasanna, wiggling out of Thamarai's grip. Another girl walked up, and Prasanna was soon deep in conversation with her, walking away from Thamarai. Thamarai stood there, hoping that Prasanna would stop and realize that she was no longer with her. But she didn't.

***

Name: Amul Babies.

Danger Classification: Harmless.

Background: Before one can understand the Amul baby entity, one must understand the rains in this area—specifically, the cyclones. Cyclone weather is beloved in this particular town because the climate becomes "chill" and the local population realizes how energetic and positive one can be when one is not drying out under a blanket of cruel heat. People drink ginger tea, frogs sing out in chorus every night, and with the right kind of handkerchief, one can catch an Amul baby.

Steps to Procurement: The best way to catch an Amul baby is to use an old kerchief, which is washed by hand every day. It must have brightly coloured edging in green, pink, orange, or red. In one corner, the kerchief must have a collection of English flowers. The kerchief may be folded into a neat square, or folded and then rolled into a tube.

Researchers have determined that the best time to catch an Amul baby is when a cyclone is due in the next three or four days. When it is particularly windy, the kerchief must be held up so that it flutters freely in the wind. Some girls have held a kerchief up for an hour, trying to catch an Amul baby. One need never lose heart though, because if one stands long enough, one will eventually succeed. This is the nature of an Amul baby: while holding up the kerchief, an imprint will appear, like someone running into an open bed sheet. At that moment, one must quickly bring the kerchief down and tie a knot on the top and bottom of the figure.

Description: Amul babies are extremely chubby, hence the name. They are vibrant, energetic, and endearing entities who enjoy being kept as pets for a short time. However, their charming nature often misleads girls, who come to believe that the Amul baby will be with them forever.

Notes on Amul Baby Attachment: Often, a girl will develop an unhealthy attachment to her entity, holding it tightly at all times as if she is clinging to something holy. She will absentmindedly stroke its head while deep in conversation. It will sit on her lap during class; the girl may even chastise her Amul baby when it misbehaves. Girls who cannot sing will croon awful lullabies to their Amul babies, and become filled with such intense feelings that they will start belching.

Once the cyclone passes, Amul babies become restless. They no longer laugh when tickled and will begin to sob loudly during the day. Girls who are familiar with Amul babies will let them go at this point, by holding the kerchief in the air until the imprint of the baby is gone. Girls who do not do this will one day look at the Amul baby and see that it has become an ordinary handkerchief again. They will stop loving it like they used to, though they may continue to sing awful lullabies for a while.

***

Thamarai never studied for anything. It was not an act of defiance. She just didn't know how to study. As far as she could tell, it involved the following tasks:

- underlining things
- memorizing things
- writing things down

Of these three, Thamarai was most adept at underlining things. She underlined things in pen and pencil, with wavy lines, single lines, and double lines with a dot at the end. The problem was that she underlined everything. She didn't like the idea of leaving some words out simply because they were considered to be unimportant. In her opinion, every word was important, and as a result every single word in her textbooks was underlined.

She was not good at memorizing. When she tried to memorize something, it would change dramatically by the time she got it into her head; chemistry equations morphed into essays on India as a growing nation, physics theorems became write-ups on Tipu Sultan. When she wrote things down, she simply wrote whatever she felt like, which meant that sometimes it was a maths formula she had made up on her own and sometimes it was just the letter 'j' over and over again.

The year was just starting, and already the entire class looked anxious and hopeless. Thamarai wanted to look anxious and hopeless as well. On a Monday, a week after 11th standard began, she decided to start studying. The first two periods were free periods, so Thamarai pulled out her Maths textbook and cracked it open, listening with dismay as the book made an actual cracking sound. She had hardly opened it till now. She saw that numerous pages hadn't even been cut and were so white they were a light blue. This was in stark contrast to Prasanna's textbooks, which always had small, neat notes written in pencil, and soft, well-thumbed pages. Thamarai had to wrestle with her textbook to keep it open, repeatedly bending it backwards to no avail. She finally slammed her bag down hard onto her desk and used it to keep the book open.

She pulled out her rough notebook, which she hadn't opened for a long time either. The first few pages were filled with the innumerable tiny dashes she drew during class. These doodles always started out benignly enough as a comma or a stray dot. But Thamarai found it difficult to leave such marks alone. Soon she would be making clouds and mazes of tiny dashes, many of them extending over multiple pages. Nobody admired them because, as S.T. Priya had once said, it made Thamarai look like a mental. But she had no time for any of that now. She unscrewed the cap of her pen and frowned down at the textbook.

A system of m linear equations in n unknowns is of the following form

$$\begin{aligned} a_{11}x_1 + a_{12}x_2 + a_{13}x_3 + \cdots + a_{1n}x_n &= b_1, \\ a_{21}x_1 + a_{22}x_2 + a_{23}x_3 + \cdots + a_{2n}x_n &= b_2, \\ \cdots \quad \cdots \quad \cdots \quad \cdots & \quad \cdots \\ a_{m1}x_1 + a_{m2}x_2 + a_{m3}x_3 + \cdots + a_{mn}x_n &= b_m, \end{aligned}$$

where the coefficients a_{ij}, $i = 1, 2, \cdots, m$; $j = 1, 2, \cdots, n$ and b_k, $k = 1, 2, \cdots, m$ are constants.

If all b_k's are zeros, then the above system is called a **homogeneous system** of linear equations. On the other hand, if at least one of the b_k's is non-zero, then the above system is called a **non-homogeneous system** of linear equations. If there exist values $\alpha_1, \alpha_2, \ldots, \alpha_n$ for $x_1, x_2, \ldots, x_n$ respectively which satisfy every equation of (1), then the ordered n-tuple $(\alpha_1, \alpha_2, \ldots, \alpha_n)$ is called a **solution** of (1).

Thamarai stared at what she had just read. She pulled out her pencil and carefully underlined all the words that were already in bold. Then she underlined all the things that did not seem like actual words. Then she underlined all the other words in case those were important too. With a small sigh, she realized that none of this was helping her understand anything. And though she tried to fight against them, questions kept erupting inside her.

Why eleven?

Why didn't they start at one?

Why *a* and then *x*?

How do you get a *b* from all of this?

Thamarai looked around. Prasanna, along with most of the other girls, was sitting outside in the corridor. Only S.T. Priya was sitting beside her, deep in conversation with another girl. There was no reason to bother S.T. Priya with her questions. She probably hadn't studied any of this either and it was very likely she would get mad if Thamarai interrupted her mid-conversation. Thamarai turned round and began poking her in the arm anyway.

"Yenna ya!" S.T. Priya snapped peevishly.

"What is this?" said Thamarai, pointing at the equation in her textbook.

"Loll-ah for you? How will I know what that is?"

"It's a system of *m* linear equations."

"Fine. Now leave me alone."

"Why *m* though?"

"Dei, don't do it."

"Just tell me that. Just that one thing."

"Why are you taking my life like this!"

"I'm just trying to understand."

"You won't understand all this. You are a mug up case."

"Don't say that."

"Then what? Why is *m* here, why is my uncle there? Who else will ask questions like this?"

S.T. Priya pointedly turned back to her conversation and Thamarai went back to her text. There was no way she could mug up what she had just read. She could already see all the *x*'s and 11s curling around each other, becoming hopelessly entangled. With a resoluteness that made her look ridiculous, Thamarai gathered her notebook, pen, and textbook, got up, and went outside. Prasanna was sitting alone at the end of the corridor, answering questions from an old exam paper. Thamarai plonked herself down beside her and smiled.

"Iru," said Prasanna, not looking up from her notebook. So Thamarai waited. She looked around at the other girls who were scattered about the hallway. To her surprise, she noticed that most of them were studying. What if what they were learning wasn't even real? What if someone had simply made everything up and slapped it together into a textbook, because it didn't matter what you taught these kinds of girls?

The thought made Thamarai feel very tired. She almost got up to leave, but Prasanna caught her arm and made her sit down again.

"Tell me," said Prasanna. "What's happening with you?"

"Nothing," said Thamarai. "I just came to waste some time with you."

"I'm answering old exam papers, want to join me?"

"Aiyyo."

"Yenna aiyyo. Come, let's do this one, physics."

"Oh, no thank you. I don't want you to feel bad when I get everything right and you don't."

"Okay, I will talk to you for five minutes. Then I will do another paper."

For a second, Thamarai forgot why she was there. Then she remembered she had been trying to study... something with an '*m*' in it? She could vaguely recall some brackets and an *x*.

"I was trying to study," Thamarai said awkwardly.

"Very good! What were you studying?" said Prasanna with genuine happiness.

"Then I came here to have a break you see."

"Oh, now I understand," said Prasanna. "Otherwise, I was thinking: this one won't come into the corridor, usually she just sits in the class."

"Yes, I have decided to study and take things seriously now," said Thamarai, shocked at the words that were coming from her mouth.

It was a novel idea: the bad student who was beyond all hope finally turning over a new leaf. Now her future would be bright, and the teachers would stop her in the hall to share their admiration. Classmates would ask her for help, and she would explain everything in an easy, clear way that they would all appreciate. She would either become a doctor or an engineer; doctor probably, because she wasn't completely sure what an engineer was. Her previous idea that they were people who made engines seemed to have been wrong.

Thamarai did not want to be a doctor. She did not like people and was not particularly interested in whether they were healthy or not. Still, this was the only other available option: she was destined to become Dr. Thamarai. It sounded silly.

"You know how happy I am to see this change in you?" said Prasanna. "I always said you were an intelligent girl, you just need to motivate yourself."

"True."

"Maybe on Saturday-Sunday you can come home and we can study together."

"Yes, why not," said Thamarai, vaguely aware that she should not be agreeing, considering that she had no intention of studying anything, even if it was at Prasanna's home.

"We can make a plan," said Prasanna, opening her notebook to its last page. She began making a table, with dates and times, empty squares to be checked once a chapter was finished. It was a nice table. Thamarai could appreciate it.

"Yenna, now you're bothering her, are you?" called a voice. S.T. Priya was striding down the corridor towards them.

"Hey, it's not like that, she has been studying," said Prasanna.

"Yah, yah, she's been studying her grandfather's bald head."

Thamarai rose and dusted off her skirt. "Okay," she said, mustering what little dignity she could. "I will go back to it now."

As she walked away, she could hear Prasanna admonishing S.T. Priya, and S.T. Priya saying that even if the skies fell down all around her, Thamarai would not study. Thamarai went to her bench, put away her books, folded her hands and sat perfectly still. She thought about physics and realized that she didn't really know what it was for. Lifting things? Calculating lifting things? Did it have something to do with springs? Thamarai sincerely wondered about this for about two seconds. Then she fell asleep.

***

Name: The Phantom First Floor.

Danger Classification: Moderately dangerous, as the floor has been known to hold people hostage if it does not want them to leave. Particularly dangerous to those who have no sugar jellies or water with them.

Description: Looks exactly like the real first floor of the GGHSS. Usually populated by various supernatural beings, or, in some cases, by nothing at all. The open corridors may extend normally or continue on into infinity. Sightings of 9D are particularly common here. Accessible only by the stairs.

The Supernatural Homeowners Association of the Phantom First Floor: Sometime in the early 90s, rumours began to spread of the formation of a Supernatural Homeowner's Association, or SHOA. This rumour was proved to be true by the appearance of a number of brochures, pamphlets, and cease and desist letters which began to thickly populate the Phantom First Floor. It is unclear who posited the idea for such an association or who the actual members were. What we do know is that the association took a very high hand in dealing with the "insurrection" of outside elements against this supernatural realm. Girls who appeared on the Phantom First Floor were immediately made to feel unwelcome, thanks to a number of strongly worded posters which appeared on all the walls. While the SHOA still technically exists, it is not clear *where* it exists, as records show that the association decided en masse to further explore one of the corridors which led to infinity, and has not been heard from since.

***

Thamarai discovered the Phantom First Floor on a hot, cloudy day. The endless free periods had become exhaustingly boring, so she had decided to go for a short walk around the school. Nobody noticed her leave the classroom. Nobody noticed her slowly meander down the corridors. She went to the school stores and bought a handful of sugar jellies. Then she decided to go upstairs.

One of the few good things in the GGHSS was its staircase. The steps were wide and close to each other, which made it feel like you were flying if you ran up fast enough. The stairwell was always cool and Thamarai enjoyed going up and down unnecessarily. There were only two flights of stairs, which is why Thamarai knew something was off when she realized she had gone up a third flight.

When she reached the Phantom First Floor, Thamarai felt a hollow feeling settle inside her. This place looked exactly like the real first floor, except that everything seemed abandoned. No part of GGHSS was ever empty; this was a school that frequently had to hold classes in the open grounds because there weren't enough rooms. And yet here was an entire floor, seemingly empty and forgotten by everyone else.

Thamarai saw that some classrooms were locked but others had their doors wide open. Each open room had a chair and table for the teacher. There were no benches, which meant these classrooms were for lower standards. The rooms had an air of waiting about them. It was as if the entire class had stepped out for a second and were due back any minute. One or two of the locked classrooms had windows that opened out into the corridor. When Thamarai peered through them, all she could see was a blackness so deep and thick she felt she could touch it.

On her left, the open side of the corridor looked down on the same courtyard. But she could not see the end of the corridor; the classrooms running down the right side seemed to go on forever. She passed one classroom which appeared to be in session, except there was no teacher. Rows of girls sat quietly on the floor, each one cross-legged and looking straight ahead. The longer Thamarai looked at them, the odder they seemed. No one moved. There was no sound, not even the odd cough or sniffle. They weren't even blinking. Thamarai kept walking, passing empty classrooms and rooms filled with piles of notebooks and old chairs. Some classrooms had white cloth covering everything, so they looked like they were filled with sleeping ghosts.

She had a feeling that she had been walking for a long time and still, the end of the corridor was not in sight. When she turned around, the corridor still stretched ahead of her. Maybe I'm not moving at all, Thamarai thought to herself. Maybe I'm just walking in place.

When she got tired, she sat with her back to the wall and ate half a sugar jelly. In one of the empty classrooms, she found a bottle, half-filled with stale, oily water. As she kept walking she noticed classrooms filled with strange things; one contained a dust storm, another a dying landscape lit by a large, red sun. One classroom appeared to be the storeroom of a shop. Bundles wrapped in brown paper lay silently on the shelves beside piles of sparkling geodes and dusty brown glass vials. Some oddly shaped objects wrapped in cloth were moving slowly, as if they were stretching. It occurred to Thamarai that if she went through this storeroom, and then left by the shop door, perhaps she could escape to some other place. But she found that she could not cross the threshold to enter, and after a number of failed attempts, she continued down the corridor.

She wondered if anyone was looking for her, how long the sugar jellies would last, and what she would eat once they were gone.

Soon, though she had been walking in one direction, in a straight line, she found herself at the staircase again. She ran down the stairs and found that everything was as she had left it. Nobody had even noticed she was gone.

After that day, Thamarai periodically found herself on the Phantom First Floor, sometimes staying there a few minutes, other times staying for what felt like weeks. From then on, whenever she left the classroom, she always carried some sugar jellies and a bottle of water with her.

***

The English Sir was tall and bespectacled, with an unremarkable moustache and a stump where his left ring finger should have been. When he walked down the hall, girls fell silent, some of them slipping away as quickly and quietly as possible. Teachers stepped aside to allow him to pass. At special school functions, he sat on stage next to the headmistress and when he was invited to say a few words, he always spoke in English. No one ever understood what he said. Most of the GGHSS teachers taught even their English medium classes in Tamil. The English Sir was one of the few teachers who taught in English. He did not approve of tuition culture. He was fiercely patriotic and actively involved with the local NSS chapter. And even though he was an atheist with a sticker on his bike that said, "There

Is No God", he came from an extremely religious and pious family, which evened things out.

He was considered to be forward thinking and open-minded, but not in a Western way. He did not like feminists and only supported a woman's right to education up to a certain point. He liked to tell a story of how he had once met some white people in town. One of the young women had lit a cigarette and asked him if he was going to object. The English Sir had simply smiled and said he had no right to say anything to her as she was a foreigner, but if she had been a Tamil woman, he would have slapped the life out of her. Sometimes he claimed that this made the foreign woman feel ashamed and she immediately put out the cigarette and apologized. Sometimes he talked about how the foreign woman was hardly wearing anything, and there was nothing left to the imagination because it was all on display.

"See any rape case with a foreign woman," he would say. "She will be dressed in similar fashion! Then what can she expect?"

Unlike the foreign woman of his story, the average middle-class conservative girl in this town lived a tightly controlled life. She did not look up from the road when she cycled and never used the cycle bell for fear of drawing attention to herself. She stayed away from boys, and from cars with tinted glass. She did not smile in public. When dressing in half saris, extra pins were used to ensure that bra straps and waists were never, ever visible. And still, when someone catcalled or groped her, it was always her fault. In this climate, the English Sir behaved in ways that may have seemed benign but always had disastrous results for the girls involved.

There were certain things about the English Sir that everyone knew. His main goal was to target and "spoil" an 11th or 12th standard girl who was pretty, unafraid, and a little unaware of herself. The tactics he used were obvious and frustrating. He would call the girl to his room and speak to her for hours, reclining in his chair while the girl stood and listened. He did this with his door open, so no one could claim that he was hiding what he was doing. He would speak casually at first, then suddenly ask something inappropriate and smirk at the girl's reaction.

"Why do you pin your half sari up there?" he would ask,

gesturing towards the girl's right breast where the half sari was always pinned to the blouse, to prevent slipping.

"Sir?"

"Why do you put a pin there? What's so precious that you have to hide it like that?"

"Sir..."

"If I tell you to take it off, what will you do?"

"No sir."

"I should make you take it off. Silly to wear so many safety pins like that. Where else do you wear safety pins, let me see."

After a while, the girl would be in his room every day, under the guise of helping him with NSS work. This too would be with the door open, so nobody could say anything. The inappropriate questions would become more frequent until soon, there would be nothing but inappropriate questions. He would read suggestive English poetry to her and then explain what it meant, to see how much she was willing to endure. When he handed her things, he would press his fingers into her palm and hold her gaze a little too long.

At some point, he would invite her home, and she would begin regularly visiting his house in the evenings, sitting with his wife and playing with his kids. He would tease her and chat while his wife prepared dinner or went to the temple. Again, the front door would always be open, to show that he had nothing to hide.

This kind of behaviour was enough to get the rumour mill going. If he was doing all this in the open, was he also pulling her into dark corners and kissing her? Was he putting his hand on her thighs when no one could see? Was he doing something worse?

Eventually, the rumours would become too much for the girl and her family to handle. She would be pulled from school and married off as quickly as possible. If she couldn't be married, she would become one of the akkas who disappeared.

There were never any consequences for the English Sir. It was completely out of the question that he should face any reprimand for his behaviour. He was respected and came from a family that was known for being respectable. It was not the English Sir's fault that he took a special interest in his some of his students. None of it was ever his fault.

The English Sir also took immense joy in making girls feel scared and uncomfortable during his classes. Everyone had to be absolutely quiet; even coughing would attract his unwanted attention. No one could move. No one could look down. Sometimes he just stood there, looking lingeringly at each girl with a slight smirk, daring one of them to do something. He enjoyed asking about their menstrual cycles. He also liked mocking local beliefs in God and rituals, particularly those connected to the menstrual cycle. He was fully aware that in most of the local castes, girls had to wash their hair every day of their period. He would spot the girls who had clearly had a head bath that morning and ask a battery of questions. "What is the occasion today? Why have you washed your hair? Anything special? Will you wash it again tomorrow? Don't be shy, tell me why you washed your hair. There must be a reason."

Some girls wouldn't say anything. Others would say "Nothing, sir" and wait till he left off questioning. But there were always a few girls who would endure it, thinking it was their fault. They would remember some family member saying it was bad to educate girls and conclude that this must be the reason why. These kinds of things wouldn't happen if they just stayed at home.

Thamarai hated the English Sir. She hated the way he dressed and how smug he was, how he could walk down any corridor and know that everyone was scared of him. She hated that people listened to him. She hated how his moustache curled over his upper lip and how he spoke English like he was better than everyone else. She hated how she had to stand barefoot in the scorching sand during assembly while he sat on the veranda in a quiet breeze, his chappals on, completely free to leave whenever he chose. She hated that he never faced any consequences. Even though he was a known porikki, he still had a wife, children, and a home, and no one thought there was anything wrong with that.

***

P. Yamuna was not a good class leader; she had simply agreed to take the post because no one else was willing. Each morning, she went to the office, where the customary two pieces of chalk and one duster were doled out to her. During assembly, she herded the class into straight lines, and when girls were being noisy, she dutifully wrote their names on a piece of paper (which would always be thrown out at the end of the period).

She would also disappear at least twice every day, only coming back a few hours later. This wasn't so unusual; with so many free periods, girls would often disappear for a while, opting to study under a tree or in a farther corridor. Teachers would periodically stick their heads into the classroom and ask why everyone was making so much noise. "Where is the class leader?" And the answer was always that P. Yamuna was nowhere to be found. No one knew where she had gone. The teacher would purse her lips and leave, and that was it.

There is a good chance that no one would have cared about all this, and things would have gone on as they did, except that one afternoon during a free period, S.T. Priya was mood out. She was often mood out, but on that day, she was particularly mood out, slouched over her desk, one arm hanging over the side, watching everyone with a slight scowl. She was so mood out that she had decided to go home after school instead of going to her grandmother's house. A teacher soon came by and asked where the class leader was. Then, without waiting for an answer, she proceeded to roast the entire class, calling them a gang of rowdies, water buffaloes, a waste of rice, and a group that were in the clutches of Sani. She wondered aloud whether there was blood running in their veins or raw sewage, and if they even ate rice at all. She asked if they had any shame, and then said they had no shame whatsoever. Why were they all here, making a din like jungle spirits? Why were they alive and ruining the lives of everyone else?

For some reason, S.T. Priya felt that the line of insults was directed only at her. When the teacher had finished her tirade and gone, S.T. Priya looked at P. Yamuna's empty seat and frowned.

"Where did that one go?" she asked. No one answered. A little while later, P. Yamuna sauntered back into the classroom, a little red and very giggly.

"Hey, where did you go?" S.T. Priya called out to her. "Do you have any idea how many teachers came and asked where you were? So many came."

P. Yamuna ignored her.

"I'm asking you a question, aren't I?" said S.T. Priya. "Do you know what kind of words that miss was yelling at us, because of you? If my people knew what kind of words I had just heard, do you know what would happen? Even I don't know what would happen."

P. Yamuna turned and looked at her."What do you want?"

"Don't do too much okay," said S.T. Priya. "I asked where you were all this time. It's because of you I had to hear such terrible insults from that teacher. I don't even know what to do now, such horrible words you never heard in your life."

"English Sir called me. Is that enough for you?"

"For so long ah?"

"What, did you miss me?" said P. Yamuna. "Did you cry because I wasn't here?"

Some girls giggled at this. P. Yamuna went back to carefully adjusting the pleats of her half-sari and S.T. Priya watched her thoughtfully.

"Yennamo something is happening," S.T. Priya said to Thamarai.

"Where?"

"All I'm asking is, are the English Sir and P. Yamuna relatives? What is there to talk about for seventeen hours every day between him and a young girl, you tell me."

"I don't—"

"With the door *closed*."

S.T. Priya did not actually know if the door was kept closed or not, but she thought it went well with the story that was beginning to form in her head.

"Door closed ah!?" said Thamarai, shocked. Like most girls, she shared a horror of men and closed doors. Being caught with anyone of the opposite sex behind a closed door signalled the demise of one's good name. The movies had also taught her that if a man gets in a room with a girl and closes the door, it generally means he is going to rape her.

"Understand what's happening now?" said S.T. Priya. "He's calling her and talking for hours with the door closed."

"What are you saying?!"

"With. The. Door. Closed!"

Soon, everyone was talking about P. Yamuna and her frequent closed-door meetings with the English Sir. Most of the girls knew for a fact that the door was never closed, but still the rumours grew. And while it was true that the English Sir was an adult and married with two daughters, it was P. Yamuna who was the guilty party here. It was her responsibility to know better, considering it was her name that would be spoiled.

The more fabrications that were added to the rumours, the more they spread. S.T. Priya decided to take it upon herself to be in charge of these matters, and ensure the rumours were always as interesting as possible.

***

Name: Aasai Candy Wrapper Time Travel.
Danger Classification: Dangerous if not handled correctly.
Description: Resembles ordinary Aasai candy wrapper.
Operating Instructions and Tips for Safe Disposal:

1. Hold one end of the wrapper.
2. Ask a friend, acquaintance, or loved one to hold the other end of the wrapper.
3. Ensure that you and the friend, acquaintance, or loved one pull on the wrapper at the same time.

The wrapper will proceed to extend to alarming lengths without tearing. The blue, yellow, and red colours will stretch and blend until nothing is left but a white length of unbreakable plastic. Normally, girls pulling on these wrappers remain where they are. But sometimes, they end up at different points in time, parallel to where they have just been. This kind of travel is almost always perilous, as these young girls often end up in tumultuous historical periods or violent settings. Many girls are killed the moment they appear in their new timeline. This causes a number of difficulties, as the girl at the other end of the wrapper will now be stuck wherever she is in time. In order to return to their correct timeline, both girls must continue to pull on the wrapper until it snaps. Since this is such a risky form of entertainment, it is generally advised that girls bury their Aasai candy wrappers deep in the ground after consumption.

***

This was a town where everything was about God. To say one didn't believe in God was in itself an act of rebellion. Gods were everywhere here. Gods were on the calendars, in the names of plastic buckets, on peanut candy wrappers. Gods were on the back windows of cars and around the necks of the local hit men. Discarded gods were collected near large trees and decorated with old garlands and dead flowers. Everyone was named after a god, even the English Sir. Gods were scattered around bus stops, banks, t-shirt shops, sweet shops, in autorickshaws, cars and on computers. Gods sat beside the posters advertising blue films, on beer labels, on tobacco packs, and in meat stalls. God was literally everywhere.

The truth was that the English Sir and his atheism were not that unique, even in this town. Almost everyone had a brother, cousin, or uncle who had somehow strayed onto paths they were not supposed to take. They had read too many English books on Marxism. They had fallen desperately in love too early in life, and when their hearts had been broken, they had spent too much time alone sitting in cremation grounds or in empty fields, contemplating life and death. They had studied abroad years ago and made friends with foreigners, but now they just sat at home, doing nothing. Families bore these young men with a mixture of exhaustion and disappointment, until they could find some hapless young woman to take over the responsibility of caring for them.

These men were disheartened in life, prone to drink, constantly planning to go to the city to make a fresh start there, but never actually leaving. Prasanna had a cousin who, years ago, had gone to the city for his first job. His name was Sanjay, and everyone—his family, his school, his college, and everyone who lived in his lane—expected great things from him. When he left, he was of marriageable age; his plan was to work in Bangalore for about six months, after which his company would transfer him to America. Sanjay had everything going for him. Accordingly, when he came home a few months later for the Deepavali holidays, the preparations for his arrival were stupendous. It was as if a young prince was coming home.

But the holidays came and went and Sanjay remained, saying he would leave for Bangalore on the weekend, then the next week, then in two weeks.

It soon became clear that he was not going back. The special foods, the bed, and the pedestal fan that had been kept just for him were withdrawn. After a year, his father kicked Sanjay out of the house. He now stayed in a spare room in Prasanna's house, taking tuition for 5th standard boys and girls. He ran errands for the family, listened to the radio, and played cricket with the children. This was probably what he would do for the rest of his life.

"Even I have advised him," Prasanna told Thamarai. "I tell him, 'Study for some civil exam, or bank exam.' How many times have I told him? You know how happy his family would be if he just took some interest?"

"Is that why he lives with you?" Thamarai asked. "Because he won't do anything?"

"Yes. Amma always had a soft spot for him, so now he is with us."

"If he gets married, everything will be alright," said Thamarai, mindlessly repeating what she had heard other adults say. She didn't really believe this. She felt it was unfair to expect a young woman to take care of a young man just because his family didn't want to deal with him anymore. Still, she knew it was the right thing to say at these moments.

"I also told him!" said Prasanna. "'Dei, Sanjay'—I always call him Sanjay, no formalities—'Dei Sanjay, at least go to the temple, see if there's any nice girl there that you like.' But what to do, he won't go to temples. He won't go anywhere. For how long can he just sit and give tuition, you tell me?"

There was a pause. Prasanna glanced at Thamarai and gave her a nudge.

"Why don't you marry him?" she said.

Thamarai immediately panicked. She had seen this young man twice and wasn't sure she wanted to see him naked, or even shirtless.

"Think about it," Prasanna went on. "He's a jolly type so he won't make you study. My house has TV, my grandmother makes nice payasam, you and I can hang out. Oh, Thamarai, it might actually be fun. Just marry him why don't you?"

The thought of spending all her time with Prasanna made Thamarai's heart skip a beat. She was sure she could put up with some shirtless fellow for that.

"But wait, you're not a Brahmin, are you?" said Prasanna. "Then leave it. If he doesn't marry a Brahmin girl that will be the last straw. They'll hire people to beat him up."

"What if he falls in love with a Musli—"

Prasanna quickly covered Thamarai's mouth with her hand.

"Don't even say it. Christian means okay, somehow, we can adjust. Muslim means my paati will have on-the-spot heart attack. Actually, my full family will have heart attack. I will be the only one left."

At that point in the conversation, Prasanna remembered that she was supposed to be studying the effects of roasting sulphide ore. She quickly chastised Thamarai for distracting her and went back to her text. Thamarai watched her study and hoped that Sanjay would find a nice Muslim girl. She hoped they would genuinely love each other and run away together on a night bus to Madurai.

***

Up until 10th standard, P. Yamuna had been pasty-faced and chubby, with a dumpy look about her shoulders. Her physical transformation in 11th standard was stunning. She went from being forgettable-looking to gorgeous almost overnight. Her eyes became darker, almost black. Her hair grew thick and long and as lustrous as a rich bolt of black silk. Her face was no longer round and pasty; strong cheekbones pushed up under her clear, firm, fair skin. To be fair, a little plump, with pitch black, thick hair—these were features all the girls wished for. P. Yamuna had all of them, and she didn't even have to try.

She carried her new beauty with complete arrogance. She knew that other girls had crushes on her. She knew some of them became tongue-tied when she spoke to them. Most people believed it was this arrogance of beauty that had made the English Sir notice her. She walked with her back straight and her head up and she looked you in the eye when she spoke. Once, to the utter horror of her classmates, she had strolled down the corridor with the end of her half-sari floating behind her.

It also seemed that P. Yamuna had become more bold. She was unafraid of the female teachers, even going so far as to walk past without greeting them. The music teacher, Punitha Miss—a poor simple woman whose hiring had been mostly an act of charity—was often bullied by P. Yamuna. Once, she had even been reduced to tears—everyone knew it was P. Yamuna's fault, but Punitha Miss would not reveal exactly what had happened.

There were two girls Thamarai had not fallen in love with: S.T. Priya, because she was S.T. Priya, and P. Yamuna, for reasons that were a mystery even to her. P. Yamuna was certainly more attractive than Prasanna, who seemed almost homely in comparison. Thamarai had tried to make herself fall in love with P. Yamuna on many occasions, but it was no use. There was something disappointing about her, something that ruined any attractiveness she may have had for Thamarai.

One day, Thamarai was more bored than usual and decided to do something different. She decided to advise P. Yamuna against the wiles of the English Sir. Thamarai thought it would be a novel, interesting thing to do. She could remind P. Yamuna that the English Sir was a filtered porikki, or something to that effect—she hadn't thought it all out yet. Whatever she ended up saying, she was sure it would be very effective. P. Yamuna would finally be cured, and the English Sir would see the error of his ways and start crying.

When Thamarai noticed that P. Yamuna was sitting by herself, she quickly went over and sat down next to her. P. Yamuna looked at her in surprise.

"Well?" said P. Yamuna.

"Has the English Sir called you?"

"Why?" said P. Yamuna, narrowing her eyes.

"Nothing. I'm just suggesting that when he calls you next, you don't go. Just you leave it."

"Leave what?"

"Think of me as your sister. Your sister is advising you."

"Eh?"

"Yes. I'm advising you like a sister."

"Oh god, what kantraavi is this."

"Who kantraavi?"

"You only."

"Why?" asked Thamarai, a little hurt.

"Why are you taking my life right now?"

"I'm not taking your life, I'm just reminding you that the English Sir is a filtered porikki. Please don't tell him I said that."

P. Yamuna was quiet.

"And if you continue like this, *your* life will get spoiled, not his," said Thamarai. "Don't spoil your life over someone like him, he's a horrid fellow anyway. Just see what he has done to so many akkas. Please don't tell him I said that."

"What? Oh, never mind," snapped P. Yamuna.

She paused for a second.

"I'm not scared of him, you know," she said suddenly.

Thamarai stared at her, unsure of what to say.

"I'm not like the rest of you, okay?" P. Yamuna continued. "He can act up as much as he wants. I'm not scared of all that."

"Who said you were scared?" said Thamarai. "He's an ass. A filtered porikki even though he's a teacher. Please don't tell him I said that."

"And what all you guys talk about me? I know about that too. I don't care about any of it. You don't know what is really happening."

The two of them sat in silence for a while. Around them, girls were talking in groups or studying. A few were taking a nap.

"I'm just saying," said Thamarai with a shrug. She was starting to get bored with the conversation.

"You don't have to say anything. I know what's going on," said P. Yamuna. She abruptly got up and left the classroom.

"Oho," called out S.T. Priya. "Someone is going somewhere."

Some girls near them said "o-HO!" in response.

Thamarai had a feeling that she hadn't said what she actually wanted to say, or that it had come out the wrong way. She thought about following P. Yamuna, maybe taking her aside and telling her properly that she was ruining her future, that this man was not a good man. But she was too lazy to get up and, considering that P. Yamuna did not even like her anyway, she thought it best to drop it altogether.

***

Name: The Rose Petal Eaters.
Danger Classification: Harmless.
Background Information: To fully understand this phenomenon, one needs to understand the cultural significance of the rose. In the GGHSS, the English rose is an exalted flower, simply because it is English. It is almost impossible to find locally. Most girls cut and keep pictures of English roses from newspapers or magazines.

There are many other flowers, but none have the same allure. The more resilient jasmine and flame of the forest are too Indian. The fickle December flower only comes out during the cold season, and the only good thing about it is that you can blow into the stem to inflate it, and then pop it against your forehead.

The paneer rose does not look like a typical rose at all, but it is close enough. These flowers are usually deep pink, and accessible year round.
Mode of Operation: It is a long-standing tradition that those in the GGHSS who choose to wear a paneer rose in their hair will immediately have it confiscated by the basketball team. It is then delicately wrapped in a handkerchief and only brought out during particularly dull classes. The petals are then carefully divided and shared by any who wish to partake. These petals are consumed delicately, only bitten and chewed with the front teeth: the tender, crisp white tip first, and finally the rest. The pieces are difficult to swallow. They stubbornly adhere to the teeth and tongue, sometimes even to the inside of the cheek, and remain there for rest of the day. Hence the name: Rose Petal Eaters.
Description: After consuming five or more petals, exquisite creepers will start to grow from the backs of the Rose Petal Eater's ears. Studded with silver thorns

and small, ruby-coloured beetles, the creepers will often snake into the girl's braid or wrap themselves around her head. There is a single recorded instance of a creeper wrapping itself around a girl's neck and trying to choke her. The creepers only last the duration of an afternoon. They can look quite stunning when adorning the right kind of head. Unfortunately, since the creepers are a supernatural phenomenon, most girls cannot see them, and they usually go entirely unnoticed.

***

The rumours about the English Sir and P. Yamuna went on blossoming like dirty flowers in all corners of the GGHSS. The more anyone spoke about them, the larger and more improbable the rumours became. Even the younger classes seemed to know that something was up with the glamorous Yamuna akka.

"So, this time what he did was," S.T. Priya explained one morning, "he closed the door. And made that P. Yamuna sit beside him while he did God knows what. And her? You think he needed to ask twice? Maanam ketta janmam."

"How did you see all that if the door was closed?" asked Thamarai.

"Why are you like this?" said S.T. Priya. "Why can't you just listen quietly?"

"Even I heard something," lied Thamarai.

"Well?" said S.T. Priya impatiently. Thamarai had admittedly not thought this through and began to think about suitably terrible things.

"Well…" said Thamarai.

"What?"

Thamarai stared blankly at S.T. Priya.

"I didn't hear anything actually," said Thamarai.

"Don't worry, it's my fault," said S.T. Priya. "I shouldn't have asked you. I forgot you're a crack. Please forgive me."

"It's okay," said Thamarai.

***

Observing the seduction of P. Yamuna and her inevitable downfall became the primary source of entertainment for 11A. It was both exciting and terrible, the idea that this girl, who was far too pretty for her own good, was being spoiled by the man who taught them English. To add a completely unnecessary layer of covertness to it all, S. T. Priya invented a set of code words for the rumours.

"Sakkara Pongal" meant there were fresh rumours (these rumours were usually that someone had seen the two talking).

"Semma Sakkara Pongal" meant that they had been seen *very, very talking*, a distinction which Thamarai did not understand.

"'Very, very talking' means?" asked Thamarai.

"Means they were talking very much. Like, *too* much," explained S.T. Priya.

"How is that different from 'talking'?"

"Means talking about unnecessary things. Like that."

"How do you know what they are talking about?"

"I know what's happening, okay?"

"How though?"

"I just understand what's happening. Anyway, mind your business," S.T. Priya said, snapping her fingers.

By now, the English Sir had successfully isolated P. Yamuna from her friends, and she had decided that this kind of isolation only happened when someone really loved you. This made her feel like she owned the world. She honestly believed that the English Sir had never treated any student like this before, that this was a true love story, different from all the other love stories out there. She believed that the English Sir would leave his wife and children, and that the two of them would move to a neighbouring town. In her mind, this was the only way the story could end. When she was older, she would tell her love story to her children, once they were able to understand.

P. Yamuna was seeing everything in this light. She now felt like everyone was rooting for her love to prevail. When other girls stared and snickered at her behind their hands, she smiled because she thought they were happy for her. Her constant state of excitement and giddiness made her more pliant as well. The girls of 11A soon discovered that during free periods, they could coax her to dance. Dancing in class, in front of other students, was the sign of a truly reckless girl, so it happened very rarely. But P. Yamuna was more than happy to dance. She only danced to one song, the current bad girl song—"Chinna Rasave Chitterembu Yenna Kadikithu". She was not a good dancer, and relied more on acting out the words while awkwardly swinging her hips. But once she was given a few words of encouragement, she was more than happy to oblige.

"Vaangeena poovum pathaathu," she would lip sync, while throwing her braid over her shoulder. Prasanna always did the real singing, while Thamarai banged along on a desk. S.T. Priya became a sort of Master of Ceremonies, telling everyone to be quiet while the dance was underway, and clapping the loudest at the end. She would egg P. Yamuna on, insisting that she was great and everyone wanted to see her dance. When P. Yamuna wasn't looking, S.T. Priya smirked at her and mimicked her movements. At the end of it all, P. Yamuna would beam.

It was just a matter of time before it all started to come apart.

***

Name: Suitcase Pasanga.

Danger Classification: Harmless.

Background Information (as reported by AMUUF volunteer 45K002): Four years ago, in 1995, a young man from Chennai came to study medicine at the local college. His parents were doctors, and had given him a second-hand white Maruti to use during his term. Unlike the other students who took buses or trains, he drove home to Chennai during the holidays. He said please and thank you to everyone, and smiled at all the young women, but not in a lecherous fashion. One day, right in the middle of term, this young man disappeared along with his car. Even after extensive searches, he could not be found. His mother continued to work but his father quit and spent his time writing letters to various politicians, government officials, and organizations, asking them to please help him find his son. Popular opinion was that the young man had run off with a girl, and the couple were now living in Bangalore.

Sometime later, it was decided to clean the polluted pond

near the GGHSS. This pond had not been cleaned in recent memory, not even when a crocodile had appeared from its depths. It was so congested with garbage and water hyacinth that the water could no longer move. The crocodile, which had mysteriously disappeared soon after its arrival, was thought to have been suffocated by the tangle of roots and filth. An earth mover was brought in, then taken away when it was realized it was of no use for dredging the pond. Instead, numerous young men dove in with buckets and machetes to haul out whatever lay down there.

That was when they found the suitcases. They were small and hardcase, containing the torsos, arms, legs, and heads of various students who had gone missing over the last few years. Most of them were North Indian students, both boys and girls, who had been cleanly dismembered and packed away with their student IDs. The sheer number of suitcases and body parts prompted the police to reopen various missing persons cases and investigate everything thoroughly. In the end, a special task force from Coimbatore discovered that the murderer was the young man with the Maruti from Chennai. He was eventually found running a soft skill and spoken English centre in Trichy.

Despite the horror and glamour of this case, it has gradually disappeared from the collective memory. The only thing that remains are the thin, sad spirits of the Suitcase Pasanga, who are now stuck near GGHSS, still under the impression that they are alive, wondering how they are going to get back to the college hostel. They mostly appear at twilight, coming up to people and asking where the nearest STD booth is. Speaking in Hindi, which most people can't understand, they try to explain that they aren't sure where they are, that their parents will be worried about them, and that the warden is sure to punish them for being off campus.

Sometimes they simply stand there, the hazy twilight shining right through them. Every so often, one of the locals will see them and stand with them, so they will not be too lonely.

(Notes, reference articles, and books for further reading provided at the back of the compendium.)

***

Not long after rumours of the affair had suffused the GGHSS, whispers began to be heard in town, in certain tuition classes and on the verandas of the older houses. On a particularly hot day, when Thamarai had just cycled home, the sisters descended on her, their eyes bright.

"Who is P. Yamuna?" they asked in unison.

Thamarai felt her heart sink. It had been a very hot day, and the last thing she wanted to do was spend her evening in the company of the sisters.

"Akkas, I'm not well," said Thamarai, slumping over awkwardly in an effort to look ill.

"What happened?"

"Periods," lied Thamarai.

"Don't be silly. You think P.T. Usha doesn't run because she has periods?"

Thamarai did not know why people always brought up the athlete P.T. Usha when talking about periods. Girls who were suffering from gut-wrenching cramps would often be told how P.T. Usha never let a little period pain stop her from achieving great things. The girls would try their best to sit in class and bear it, after which they would faint and have to be taken home.

"Come home now and tell us, amma is also waiting to hear," said the sisters. Thamarai gasped and took a step back.

"But periods," she said pleadingly.

The sisters looked at her with pursed lips. "Okay," they relented. "But first you tell us, who is P. Yamuna?"

Thamarai sighed and decided she would just say the whole thing in one go.

"P. Yamuna is our class leader," began Thamarai. "And the English Sir teaches English."

"We know who he is," said the sisters sourly. "What is he doing with P. Yamuna?"

"Right now?"

"Oh God, stop being annoying! What is happening between the two of them?"

Thamarai frowned in thought.

"I don't know," she said finally.

"What are people saying then? What is he doing to her?"

"I don't know," Thamarai said again. "I can give you facts, that's all."

The sisters looked at her hungrily and gathered close. "Tell, tell," they said in low, excited voices.

"Well," repeated Thamarai, "P. Yamuna is our class leader. And the English Sir teaches English."

The three of them seemed to look at each other for a long time. Thamarai felt like she should say something more but did not want to fracture the delicate web of silence that had formed among them. Here they were, frozen in this moment. She was strangely moved by it.

"If you're going to be like that," said the sisters stiffly. The spell shattered, and Thamarai watched as they turned rather huffily and walked back to their house. She waited until their door was firmly closed. Then she went inside.

***

Name: The Crusades (containing the Karisal Kaattu Black Holes and the Early Morning Demon).
Danger Classification: Moderately dangerous.
Description: An open ground behind the school littered with green bushes and shrubs that are known to painfully grab at arms and legs, leaving deep scratches.
Background Information: It must first be noted that the GGHSS does in fact have a set of bathrooms, six stalls to be exact. These toilets were built with special government funding, with a sign stating as much painted on one of the walls. These bathrooms are kept locked at all times. Even when it is raining hard and girls urgently need to pay a visit, they are not permitted to use these bathrooms. Instead, they are made to use the open ground behind the school in an exercise that has earned the grim name of The Crusades.
Mode of Operation: Trying their best to stay hidden, the girls must squat behind the bushes, lift their skirts, and try to pee as fast as they can. Those who are lucky will find that they are hidden completely by the bushes. Those who are not lucky—and most of them aren't—will start to pee and then notice that they have somehow completely

exposed themselves to the local train running across the nearby tracks. One of the more alarming features of The Crusades is the sudden appearance of clouds of large cockroaches that quickly swarm over the girls' feet. It is unclear if this too is a supernatural event or just the result of the area's terribly low standards of cleanliness. Researchers may investigate this phenomenon and provide notes accordingly. It may be supposed that the task of returning to class would be a relatively easy one; unfortunately, girls are likely to face more treacherous supernatural entities on their way back.

Karisal Kaattu Black Holes: The most common element to present itself during The Crusades are the Karisal Kaattu Black Holes, which shouldn't even be here in the first place. While endemic to the Karisal Kaattu region of Tamil Nadu, these black holes have often appeared on The Crusade grounds and swallowed girls. The only way in which they can be avoided is to keep an ear open for a low buzzing sound. Once this is heard, the girl or girls must make an immediate left turn and run, without looking back.

Early Morning Demons: Like the Karisal Kaattu Black Holes, the Early Morning Demons do not really belong here either. While Early Morning Demons are elsewhere found only between the hours of four and six a.m., in the GGHSS, an Early Morning Demon may be found at any time of day. This unsavoury supernatural element will try to engage a girl in conversation, often while she is peeing. It will then hound her while she tries to exit the grounds. If the girl makes the mistake of engaging with it, she too will turn into a demon. The only way to avoid this entity is to ignore it completely.

Special Note: It is clear that only the very brave, or those that *really* need to pee, can participate in The Crusades. Everyone else holds it in until they get back home in the evening, thus resulting in an abnormally high number of urinary tract infections among GGHSS students.

***

One morning, P. Yamuna came bounding into class, announcing in breathless, bubbly spurts that the English Sir was going to take a double period with them that afternoon.

"What?" asked S.T. Priya. "Why??"

"English Sir said we are just wasting time and not studying," said P. Yamuna. "So, he has decided to take class for us instead."

"For *two hours*?!"

The entire class began muttering and shifting around uneasily. Some girls hid bags that had prominent displays of gods or temples on them. Others quickly rearranged their half-saris so no skin or bra straps could be seen. Some even went so far as to remove their bindis and hide them in their geometry boxes.

"You only did this!" S.T. Priya yelled at P. Yamuna. "You told him to come."

Some of the others looked at P. Yamuna, waiting for a reply. Her face was still pink as she readjusted her half-sari, letting the end of her daavani trail behind her.

"She did this," S.T. Priya hissed at Thamarai. "She wanted to flirt with him in front of us, that's why she's doing this. She has no shame. It's become that bad. Saakada kootum."

Thamarai felt strangely energized at the prospect of the English Sir taking class. It would give her an opportunity to glare at him. Meanwhile, the class settled into their places and sat with their faces forward. It seemed like they were all wearily waiting for something terrible to happen.

Soon the English Sir came striding in. He tossed a book onto the teacher's table, folded his arms, and leaned against it, staring at the class, letting his gaze linger on some of the shyer girls. A slight smirk played on his lips. Nobody moved, except P. Yamuna, who pulled out a pen, and then rummaged in her bag for a notebook. The English Sir looked at her.

"Finished?" he asked. A flush of red splashed across her face as she quickly nodded. The English Sir turned back to the class and Thamarai watched in horror as P. Yamuna pulled a face at him and silently giggled.

He turned and wrote the word RESERVATION on the blackboard.

"What does it mean?" he said. "Prasanna don't answer."

The class was silent.

"You have travelled by train, no?"

"Yes sir," came a weak, collective answer.

"Then you must have seen? Or are you too busy eating rice to see such things?"

"Yes sir," said the class, even though they probably meant "no".

"If you have reservation, who can sit in your seat? Only you can sit. If someone sits, they will get it nicely. Correct-ah?"

"Yes sir."

The English Sir pursed his lips and switched to Tamil.

"And who knows why, but life forms like you are given reservation in education and jobs. As if you are going to become doctors and engineers. Isn't it? Don't say 'yes sir' like a bunch of idiots."

The class gaped at him, unsure of what to do.

"Do you know how many boys want to study but can't?" said the English Sir. "I personally know about four or five. Either there's no money at home or they have to go to work. Many people simply don't have the means to educate their boys, you know. But we don't hear about that because it's only important for girls to study, right? Only *you* should have everything already set aside for you, whether you deserve it or not. Concession, free uniform, free textbook. They are even giving you free food now, isn't it? Who knows why, but there it is."

He was referring to the Noon Meal Scheme, which provided sambar rice and a boiled egg to girls who couldn't afford to bring lunch. Thamarai wasn't a fan of this scheme because the Noon Meal Scheme girls ate their lunch while sitting on the cycles in the cycle stand, leaving behind large gobs of sticky rice on the handlebars and seats. However, the Noon Meal Scheme was also notorious for having lizards fall into the food and making everyone sick, so there seemed to be some sort of balance at work.

"You waste students get all that and see how well you study," he continued. "Are you worth it at all? Better to give the reservation to some water buffaloes, don't you think? They at least will give something in return."

By now, each time the English Sir looked the other way, P. Yamuna was pulling faces at him. She was tapping her forehead in frustration like he was being stupid. She was twitching her mouth in irritation. She lifted one shoulder and turned her head, like she was angry at him. She was pulling every face that the spoiled heroines in movies made when trying to rile up the hero.

Thamarai decided to ignore her. She kept her eyes fixed on the English Sir as he went on and on and *on* about the dangers of feminism. She narrowed her gaze and held her mouth in a small, grim line. She thought about his stupid moustache and his stupid half-finger. He was looking particularly stupid today, wearing dark brown trousers and a short-sleeved white shirt.

Thamarai blinked. She had noticed something out of the corner of her eye.

The old botany notebook was sticking out of her bag.

Thamarai hadn't thought about it for some time. She couldn't understand why it was sticking out of her bag; had she pulled it out? She was pretty sure she hadn't. Had someone else taken it out and hastily tried to put it back? She didn't even know why she still had it. She must throw it away soon, for real. This time she would really drop it into the drainage canal, no matter what anyone said. Imagine hanging onto something like that for so long!

"Stand up."

Thamarai frowned; she could see scribbles and drawings on the cover. They definitely hadn't been there before. There was something that looked like a hand-drawn map running along one side. On the other side, lines of numbers had been written, then crossed out. Someone had drawn a picture of the Indian flag in the bottom corner.

"What's her name? Thamarai. Are you deaf? Stand up."

Thamarai blinked.

"Did you wash your hair today?" said the English Sir. "Did water get in your ears, is that why you can't hear anything?"

Thamarai knew this was supposed to embarrass her, implying that she was menstruating. She dully remembered that she hadn't bled for a long time. In fact, she was sure her periods had stopped soon after coming to this town. She had a vague idea that this was not healthy but had never mentioned it to anyone. It was one of her secrets, along with the fact that there were huge blooms of fungus that grew around her groin and on her stomach. These too had started after moving here. She had a feeling that this was not healthy either, but it bothered her less than not menstruating.

"Didn't I tell you to stand up?" said the English Sir.

Thamarai quickly got up but was determined to keep glaring at him.

"You have Madras Eye?"

"No sir."

"What's wrong with your eyes?"

"Nothing sir."

"What were you looking at over there?"

"Over where, sir?"

She continued to glare, but it did not feel as effective as she would have liked. The English Sir had a grim look on his face.

If Thamarai had been a more intelligent girl, she would have remained silent. Instead, she decided to explain herself.

"Sir somebody put a notebook in my bag," said Thamarai. "Meaning, it's my notebook only. Actually, it's not… but *I* put it in my bag. I didn't steal it."

"What?" said the English Sir, frowning. "What's that?" P. Yamuna was still making faces and giggling. Thamarai took a deep breath.

"Sir, sometime in 9th standard actually I found this notebook but couldn't throw it away."

"What's wrong with you? Why are you talking about 9th standard?"

"You can see the notebook if you like."

"Oh, may I? Really?"

"Yes sir. I mean no sir. Not if you don't want to. I was just saying, sir."

Thamarai glanced over at P. Yamuna. Now she was staring at Thamarai too, like everyone else was.

"A-da!" said English Sir with mock interest. "Now you're looking over there. Is there a notebook there too? Shall I check for you?"

"If you want to, sir," said Thamarai. "I mean, I don't know, sir. There are some notebooks there. I didn't put them there. They aren't mine, sir. I don't know anything actually, sir."

The exchange could probably have gone on forever this way, but the bell rang. The English Sir paused, like he was trying to think of an appropriate punishment for Thamarai. But then he turned and swiftly left the classroom. Once he was safely gone, P. Yamuna stuck her tongue out and waggled her head.

"Enough with all that," S.T. Priya snapped at her. "No one thinks it's cute. And you," she said, turning to Thamarai. "Are you a crack? I'm serious, has it finally happened? Have you gone full mental?"

Prasanna turned and looked at Thamarai, and for a second, Thamarai was worried she had done something wrong again and would have to apologize to the English Sir.

"What are you playing at now?" Prasanna asked Thamarai.

"Hey really," said Thamarai, pulling the mysterious record notebook out of her bag. Parts of its spine fell away, and a cloud of dust flew up.

"Chee," said Prasanna. "Someone's record note from 1937? Throw it out, who knows what's living in it."

"And you know I have wheezing. Are you mad?" demanded S.T. Priya. There was no dustbin in the classroom and Thamarai could not think of where one might be in the rest of the school. She put the book back in her bag and decided to get rid of it on her way home.

***

Name: Smiling Face.

Danger Classification: Harmless.

Description: Smiling Face manifests when a girl is standing alone in the late afternoon sun, the jasmines in her hair browned from the heat, with beads of sweat adorning her upper lip. The girl's mind is more or less empty at this time, barring perhaps the visual of a small bird in the sky, or the sudden memory of an afternoon spent eating ripe clusters of Madras thorn. Smiling Face always appears silently, accompanied by the scent of hot metal and melted sugar. This entity has a small body made of tin and an enormous round head with painted eyes. Smiling Face has the uncanny ability to flip the top of its head all the way back, revealing worlds inside. This is only done once Smiling Face has identified a girl that it would like to add to its collection.

While many researchers have witnessed the flipping of Smiling Face's head, few have seen the types of worlds that have been revealed therein. There have been reports of girls seeing entire civilizations falling into ruin, with immense, ugly flowers rising towards the hot sky from Smiling Face's open head. Sometimes there is nothing at all. Others have beheld worlds made of water, worlds containing strings of hot glass that periodically shift into complex life forms, or worlds filled with dust and dead seeds.

Mode of Operation: Smiling Face will appropriate any girl who has looked inside its head. It is considered one of the more pleasant ways to go missing, as being with Smiling Face can be a very drowsy, warm experience, and the entity demands very little of the girls once they have been taken. In fact, it is quite easy to interview these girls after they have crossed over. Hence, we request researchers and especially our volunteers not to submit any more interviews of Smiling Face girls, as we already have too many. We also do not require any more entries on the alleged Smiling Face versus AMUUF feud, and the ensuing false reports that AMUUF conceded defeat because it was a "scaredy-pants". The event alluded to was a trifling matter and certainly has no place in this respected compendium.

Smiling Face is one of the few supernatural entities—if not the only one—to take care of those it has appropriated. The girls it abducts are always well-fed, mentally well-nourished, and filled with love for their school and their mother tongue. This is why the phrase "Always be with Smiling Face" is often used as a blessing at the GGHSS.

***

P. Yamuna's behaviour and Thamarai's flabbergasting dialogue during the English Sir's class almost drove S.T. Priya crazy. Shortly afterwards, as the June monsoons were about to set in, S.T. Priya became one of the first girls to contract Madras Eye and insisted it was due to the stress from the whole incident.

What were the two of them thinking, acting like clowns when the English Sir was just looking for an excuse to be a psycho? He was not a normal teacher. Did they want him to go full-crazy on all of them? How could S.T. Priya *not* contract Madras Eye with such things going on?

"Best to keep all this behaviour to yourself," S.T. Priya said loudly, so the whole class could hear. By then her Madras Eye was in full bloom. She wore dark glasses in class, and the girls had taken to calling her Karu Uncle. She spent the days leaning against the wall, periodically breaking into song while dabbing at the tears that continuously rolled down her cheeks. The itchiness of her eyes was directly linked to her self-righteous tirades against P. Yamuna. Though these had become more frequent, they were never aimed at P. Yamuna directly; S.T. Priya was too much of a coward for that. Instead, she launched her tirades at anyone who happened to be near, usually Thamarai.

"Look here," she said. "We don't need anyone acting like a clown when that man comes. Why should we get in trouble because someone wants to act like a crack? The rest of us can't behave that way and get away with it, like *some* people can."

Thamarai, who had not been paying attention to anything S.T. Priya was saying, looked up and caught her breath. Two rows away, P. Yamuna was looking particularly dazzling, with the late afternoon sun spilling across her face. Her dark hair glistened and her eyes seemed to glow with a deep richness. Everything about her was bewitching. For a second, Thamarai thought she might fall in love with P. Yamuna after all. But the feeling quickly faded.

"That's all I am saying," said S.T. Priya. "Do whatever you want, it's not my affair. That that man, that that business. But don't drag the rest of us—"

P. Yamuna turned towards S.T. Priya and narrowed her eyes.

"What exactly are you talking about? What do you mean?" she said.

For a second, S.T. Priya was taken aback. She hadn't expected a response, least of all from P. Yamuna herself.

"What do you mean, what do I mean?" said S.T. Priya, unable to think of anything else to say.

"What did you mean by 'like some people can'?" said P. Yamuna.

"You know what."

"Tell."

S.T. Priya looked uncomfortable.

"I don't have to tell anything. Everyone knows what I mean," she said.

"If you have any guts, tell. What are you talking about and who are you talking about?"

Thamarai looked at S.T. Priya with genuine curiosity. She had no idea how S.T. Priya was going to answer this one without looking absolutely stupid. Thamarai wanted to see what she came up with.

For a second, S.T. Priya didn't say anything. Then she looked around her, letting her gaze linger menacingly on Thamarai.

"That's right all of you, sit there and stare," said S.T. Priya. "You all know how to come and ask for sakkara pongal when you want it, right? For that you guys are all ready to come. But when P. Yamuna asks you point blank, suddenly you don't know anything."

"Very good," said Thamarai.

"Yenna, very good?" S.T. Priya snapped at Thamarai. "You too. You know how to ask when you want some gossip, right? Right?"

"When have I asked you for sakkara pongal?" said Thamarai. "I'm not even sure what that means." It was true. Apart from Prasanna, Thamarai was the only one in the class who didn't participate in the rumours. This was not due to any lofty ideas of right and wrong. It was only because Thamarai's mind tended to wander during gossip, so she never really caught onto what was being said.

"Hey," said P. Yamuna, looking at S.T. Priya. "I asked you, not them. You give me an answer."

"Oh, I see," said S.T. Priya, looking at everyone except her. "Now I understand what kind of people you are. Well? P. Yamuna asked a question, no? Why don't one of you answer her?"

Thamarai was smiling at P. Yamuna, who was really looking so beautiful in that rich, yellow sunlight. Maybe that was what prompted her to do what she did.

"She is talking about you and the English Sir," Thamarai said helpfully. "And how you two are behaving indecently and having an affair."

There was a stunned silence. It felt like the entire class was holding its breath.

"I never said they were having an affair, you ass!" gasped S.T. Priya.

"Seri. You are just behaving indecently then," clarified Thamarai.

P. Yamuna stared at S.T. Priya, who appeared to be staring back, though it was difficult to tell with the dark glasses. The rest of the girls looked on in silence. P. Yamuna's face was stony and difficult to read. S.T. Priya became very interested in the contents of her school bag.

Then Kayalvizhi Miss, the maths teacher, came in, and a double period of maths began. Thamarai kept looking back and forth from one girl to the other, so often so that Kayalvizhi Miss asked what was wrong with her. The tension in the class was still palpable, almost a visible line connecting P. Yamuna and S.T. Priya. Surely something would erupt after class.

But when school ended that day, P. Yamuna left quickly. Several girls stayed back, taking time over packing their bags, hoping something interesting would happen. Thamarai stayed back as well, under the impression that someone was distributing snacks.

"You only," said S.T. Priya to Thamarai. "You only! What kind of idiot says something like that? Right in front of her?"

"Oh, that's nice," said Prasanna. "What has she done wrong? Whatever you all were whispering to each other, she said aloud. You guys can talk about it, but she can't?"

Many voices overlapped each other. They reminded Thamarai of a snarl of bicycles that had become entangled by the handlebars. S.T. Priya found herself fumbling.

"But there's a limit, isn't there?" said S.T. Priya.

"Exactly," said Thamarai.

"See this clown. Yenna exactly?" said S.T. Priya. "We're talking about you! Why did you say that to P. Yamuna?"

Thamarai pursed her lips thoughtfully. "What did I say?" she wondered, mostly to herself.

"Aiyyo! Why are you like this?" said S.T. Priya. "And don't

say 'like what', I will scream."

S.T. Priya was having a difficult day, Thamarai thought. Even with her eyes hidden behind cooling glasses, you could tell that she was exasperated, worried, and angry.

Prasanna put away her books and stood up sharply. "Thamarai! Come, let's go," she said. Thamarai felt a pleasant tingle run through her.

"Come." Thamarai picked up her bag. She said a general bye to everyone, took out her cycle key, and followed Prasanna out of the classroom. The sun hung low on the horizon, and she could see that most of the cycles were already gone from the cycle stand. A few ragged 6th standard girls wandered around, picking up dropped keys, pens, and handkerchiefs. As the sunlight winked in tones of peach and pink, a gigantic pale yellow worm slowly crested the surface of the sand and gently shook its back. The 6th standard girls were all knocked over, tumbling to the ground in a blur of dark green and white. Then they picked themselves up and kept scouring the sand for lost items. The sand worm lay in the sun for a few seconds, its thin red eyestalks waving from side to side, and then submerged itself again. No one saw any of this except Thamarai.

***

Name: The Sex Demon.
Danger Classification: Harmless.
Misconceptions Regarding the Name: One of the many entities to emerge from the Supernatural Cine Explosion of 1987, the Sex Demon's existence is shrouded in confusion and misinformation. The most common misconception is that they are responsible for sex—or rather, sexual misconduct—particularly the kind practiced by certain male members of society. In actuality, the Sex Demon has absolutely nothing to do with sexual matters. It neither causes nor encourages acts of sexual abuse. In fact, some researchers are of the opinion that the Sex Demon knows absolutely nothing about sex, a theory bolstered by the fact that they have no sexual organs whatsoever.

Description: The Sex Demon resembles those villains from Tamil movies of the seventies and eighties who were inclined to rape women at the drop of a hat. Both the Sex Demon and these villains take a great deal of pride in their choice of dress, alternating between Western and ethnic wear, wearing both with aplomb and enthusiasm. When they opt for Western clothing, Sex Demons prefer pale blue three-piece suits with suspenders, hat, brown shoes, and shiny gold glasses. They also enjoy smoking a pipe. When they are in the mood for ethnic wear, Sex Demons prefer silk white jubbahs with silk white veshtis, gold bracelets, and tiger tooth pendants.

Mode of Operation: The Sex Demon is an agrarian entity, taking a strong interest in the growth of native rice strains, millets, vegetables, and fruits. It is not uncommon for one or more Sex Demons to maintain a small garden plot. Apart from gardening work, the Sex Demon does very little else. Left to themselves, Sex Demons enjoy sitting in large, colourful, uncomfortable houses. They like holding dirty glasses containing whisky while clenching their pipes between their teeth. They are also fond of repeating the following lines under their breath, when they think no one can hear them:

Kottampatti rotile
Kutti pora pokile
Kuttiya thaan paapena
Rotiya thaan thinbena

At the GGHSS, there are at least four documented Sex Demons that live in the botany and chemistry labs. There are rumours of more that reside in the main building, but they seem to keep to themselves. They are harmless, and do not enter willingly into human lives.

***

Prasanna was quiet on the way home. She went slowly, so Thamarai could keep pace with her TVS, but she hardly said a word. Thamarai tried to be charming, telling some of her best jokes, but nothing seemed to work. Prasanna was deeply preoccupied; her brow was furrowed and her lower lip had disappeared. She barely even acknowledged that Thamarai was there.

When they reached the tracks, the railway gate was coming down, so they dismounted. But Prasanna was not in the mood to duck under it and run across as usual. Instead, they both stood there in silence, waiting for the train to pass, the evening sun dappling their shoulders. Thamarai did not like this change in Prasanna's behaviour. She felt she must have done something to make her angry, but when she asked about it, Prasanna shook her head.

"Nothing like that da," said Prasanna. "If you go home a little late, will your aunt say anything?"

"No, why?"

"Then come home for a few minutes," said Prasanna.

Thamarai nodded. A movie at the local soft porn theatre was just ending, and a swarm of sweaty men poured onto the street. One of them stuck his arm out, hoping to touch Thamarai's breast as she cycled past, but she deftly swerved to avoid him. Prasanna rode slightly ahead of Thamarai, who was getting more and more uncomfortable. She did not anticipate anything terrible happening, but she wondered if Prasanna was going to give her a long talk about the future and how to prepare for life. In which case, Thamarai would much rather go home and face the sisters.

When they reached Prasanna's house, Thamarai parked her cycle near the gate while Prasanna walked her TVS to the side of her house. Prasanna then went to get some water. Thamarai sat on the wooden bed that was kept on the veranda. They drank the tepid water in silence and Thamarai looked at Prasanna's hands, the fall of her skirt over her knees. Prasanna had the telltale GGHSS shoulder slump, born from years spent sitting cross-legged on the floor and looking up at the teacher. Her shoulders looked even more slumped than usual. It was the first time Thamarai had seen Prasanna look dejected, and it was unnerving. Prasanna was usually the optimistic one, the one who was willing to try to find a way forward. Now it looked like she was defeated by everything.

"She's just spoiled her life," said Prasanna. "All because of that porikki. Imagine spoiling your life for someone like that!"

Thamarai could not imagine it. There was something about the English Sir that reminded her of empty wasps' nests and plastic bottles filled with kerosene; of everyday, depressing things. She could think of nothing that would induce her to sit near him on a bus or stand beside him in a government office. He seemed harsh and empty, with no promise of anything good.

"Don't you feel like doing something?" asked Prasanna.

"About what?" said Thamarai.

Prasanna paused.

"About P. Yamuna," she said. "She's our classmate after all, right? And her life is getting spoiled. What do I mean *getting* spoiled... it's already spoiled."

But what could anyone do? Thamarai wondered. Even the English Sir could not make this go away. It had happened, and everyone who knew about it would carry it in some way for years.

"I think someone should talk to her," said Prasanna. "Can't do anything about *him*. But someone should advise *her*."

"I tried once," said Thamarai. "But she wouldn't listen."

"Someone has to *do* something."

"What do you think can we do? We are not Vijayashanthi. We are not someone important."

Prasanna paused again, then sighed.

"I mean, what could P. Yamuna do, even?" said Thamarai. "That porikki calls her to his room. What can she do? Say no?"

Prasanna was staring at something on the ground, thinking hard. Thamarai began to fidget. She was no longer interested in the conversation; she wanted to go home. She remembered the record notebook sitting in her bag and thought about throwing it out on the way. Maybe she could even throw it out here, at Prasanna's house. She knew there was a small, plastic dustbin in the hall. She decided she would throw it out before she left.

"There is nothing we can do," said Prasanna. She looked genuinely upset.

"It's just because we are no one," said Thamarai gently. "What can you do when you are no one?"

Prasanna kept staring at the ground.

"P. Yamuna has too much headweight anyway. That's why he caught her," said Thamarai. This was the only thing she could think of to justify what was happening. She thought of the arrogant things that P. Yamuna had done, how she had made Punitha Miss cry, and tried to convince herself that P. Yamuna deserved it all. Things like this didn't happen unless the girl was willing. Things like this only happened to a certain kind of girl. And P. Yamuna was that kind of girl.

That was how Thamarai resolved it in her head.

She pulled out her cycle key and got up. Prasanna remained seated on the veranda. When Thamarai said bye, Prasanna only looked at her for a moment. Then she nodded her head. Thamarai made her way home, thinking about their conversation. *It's not like any of us are friends with P. Yamuna. Why are we feeling responsible?* She cycled slowly, watching the daylight fade and the twilight mosquitoes settle on her arms. It was only when she was almost home that she realized that she had forgotten to throw out the record notebook again.

***

Name: The Cine Hero.
Danger Classification: Dangerous.
Description: Another entity born of the Supernatural Cine Explosion of 1987, the Cine Hero is one of the most deadly entities in the GGHSS. He exists in the shadows, in corners, under the stairs, at the backs of classrooms, and in any other place that is dark and out of the way. If a girl wanders too close to one of these places, the Hero will appear; and from that point, the girl is irretrievably lost. The Hero will be named Suresh, Raj, or Usman. His hair will be dry and combed back, his moustache harmless but manly. He will wear a long-sleeved white shirt, modestly buttoned at the wrists. He will also wear a thick, white veshti, though he will wear lungis at home. When he wears a lungi, he will hold it up at his crotch. When he wears a veshti, he will lift his heel, scoop up the hem, and tie it around his waist. He will not wear any gold, though he probably could if he wanted to.
Mode of Operation: The Hero's courtship will be silent and filled with gentle longing. When the hapless girl looks up, she will see him leaning against the wall, his eyes

brimming with tears as he gazes at her. Once she starts leaning against walls herself, he will stand in the shadows where she can't see him, and gently take her hand from around the corner. In this way, the girl will believe she is experiencing feelings of love, longing, adoration, and sexual desire. In truth, the Hero is starting to insinuate himself into her body, fingers first. The girl will become perpetually tired. She will only drink water. She will linger in the corners of hallways. She will calculate how many plastic buckets, stainless steel plates, tumblers, and straw mats they will need to buy for the new house. She will decide who she will buy milk from, and what kind of shampoo she will use on a regular basis. She will always settle on Clinic Plus. Once, and only once, a feeling like an orgasm will wrack her body, and she will give a very small yelp. This signifies that the Hero is now leaving her. He will abandon her as a husk of a girl with her mouth open, as if she is surprised that it finally came to this. These husks always blow away eventually.

***

The record notebook remained in Thamarai's bag. Every time she tried to throw it out, she would put it back in her bag without realizing it. One afternoon, when everyone was sitting out in the corridors, Thamarai pulled it out and placed it carefully in front of her. She had never taken a really good look at it.

It was not from 1937. In fact, dates written on several of the pages showed that it was only a few years old; and yet it was extremely weathered and battered. Small shelves of dust had settled on the pages and in the binding. The dust was so fine that it seemed to slip into Thamarai's skin whenever she touched it. The notebook also seemed to be home to a number of silverfish. There was one in particular, a large and oddly coloured one, that kept bothering Thamarai. She did not have any special hatred for silverfish, but this one annoyed her greatly. It sat in the binding of the book, tucked far enough in that it was impossible to reach. When she tried to shoo it out of the binding, it would either not move at all, or else it would slowly crawl deeper inside. The one time she had managed to prod it with her fountain pen, it had twisted its body sharply, as though in pain. Due to its size, and the fact that its colouring was so brilliantly silvery that rainbows danced constantly over its body, Thamarai believed that this silverfish was a very ancient one. She could not get rid of it. She had whacked it with at least three of her textbooks, her bag, and S.T. Priya's geometry box to no avail.

There were also a number of much tinier silverfish, so small that it was difficult to see them. They dotted the pages, sitting there motionless until Thamarai accidentally touched them, sending a streak of silver and rainbows across the page. She spent one afternoon trying to smear as many as she could, but the next day they were all back again.

The first few pages of the notebook had the usual transection drawings of shoeflowers and coat-button flowers. It was what was written in the rest of the notebook that was curious. Whenever she tried to show it to someone, the person would either refuse to look, or else they would take a passing glance and shrug, saying it looked like a normal botanical entry—though no one would ever actually read it. When Thamarai tried to copy one of the entries, she kept writing gibberish in a mix of Tamil and English. She had the idea of taking a closer look at the text, but it kept slipping away, literally sliding down the page in a cascade of letters. She even tried keeping her finger on the words, to prevent them from moving, but they still kept shifting, sometimes becoming so hazy that she couldn't tell what she was looking at. It was only when she wasn't focused on the text that she found she could read it.

The entries seemed to be about forlorn entities who, for some reason, were stuck in or around her school. The longer she sat with the book, the more she began to understand its words. She realized that she had actually seen several of the listed entities before, but had convinced herself that she hadn't. She clearly remembered seeing the Sand Worm of Patriotism several times. And she had often noticed small, well-tended squares or rectangular plots of healthy vegetation in the oddest places—she now realized these were the gardens of the Sex Demons. She remembered seeing a tin entity standing with its mouth open, ready to swallow the sky. And, of course, the

Paati—though she had seen that at S.T. Priya's house, not at school. These things, which she had tried to forget, or which she convinced herself were figments of her imagination, were real. Even though no one else could see them, there was proof of it now, right in her hands.

***

Name: The Little Nightmares.
Danger Classification: Dangerous.
Description: The GGHSS has always had a Nightmare problem. The Nightmares were there long before the school was created, and unlike other native entities, they have never faded or dissolved. They are either found alone or in clusters, usually clinging to ceiling fans or in the corners of sparsely used rooms. It is unclear what these entities are made of, though they often resemble bubbles or balloons. Their colour may vary but they are always of a smoky hue, as if they have been dusted with powdered sugar. While the Little Nightmares do not set out to camouflage themselves, they often go unnoticed and can stay dormant for years at a time if left alone.
Mode of Operation: Once disturbed, a Little Nightmare will aggressively follow its life cycle until it is time for it to go into stasis once again. If meddled with, they attach themselves onto the host and become utterly impossible to remove. The new host will have no option but to accept the supernatural parasite and prepare for the worst.

On initial exposure to the host, the entity will begin to take root in the brain and heart, causing small visions or nightmares which are only mildly unpleasant but completely absurd. The way to defeat these nightmares entirely is to ignore them from the start; but therein lies the problem, for one cannot know there is a Little Nightmare infestation until it is well advanced and deeply rooted in the host.

As the infestation worsens, the Little Nightmares will become longer and take on a distinctly personal flavour. They will start to embody the person's real fears and anxieties, keeping the host frozen for minutes at a time. They will feel intensely real, and the host won't be able to stop thinking of them, even when awake. Soon, the host will become paralysed for hours at a stretch, often just sitting with eyes wide open, mesmerized.

The final stage of the infestation will involve almost continuous personal nightmares, drawn from things that have happened in the past and those which the host fears may happen in the future. Based on available memory and language, the Little Nightmares will continuously create new nightmares. By this time, the host will have nothing left inside. They may carry on living, but their eyes will be empty. When asked about likes or dislikes, they will be unable to answer. They will also begin to disappear from the sight and minds of their loved ones so that by the time the final stage begins, everyone has forgotten about them anyway.

During the final stage, nothing can be done for the host. They will slowly develop a round, chitinous covering with a dusty colouring and balloon-like appearance. Soon, this new Little Nightmare will go off to nest in a corner or near a ceiling fan, until it is disturbed.

***

Thamarai learned about the supernatural entities and areas in the GGHSS in fits and starts. There were some phenomena with which she never interacted at all; for instance, since she never peed at school, she avoided The Crusades. She never experienced Aasai Candy Wrapper Time Travel because she did not eat Aasai candies. Other entities were large and overpowering, like the Phantom First Floor. In these instances, she was simply carried along, and there was not much she could do about it.

Other supernatural entities were relatively harmless to interact with. The Amul Babies were sweet though short-lived. On one occasion Thamarai had met one of the Suitcase Pasanga, and though they had spoken mostly in Hindi, she liked to believe she understood some of what they said.

The Little Nightmares proved to be different. For some

reason, they did not work on Thamarai. She found her first cluster on the Phantom First Floor. In one of the classrooms, the tables were almost overrun with them. They seemed harmless, almost like gigantic foreign candies, and Thamarai could not help herself from breaking off a small, lavender-coloured nightmare. It immediately attached itself to the underside of her thumb. Nothing happened. Later, when Thamarai learned a bit more about the Little Nightmares, she wondered if the reason she didn't freeze up was simply that they had nothing to work with, given that her usual state of mind was one of depression and diluted awareness anyway.

She kept the Little Nightmare on her thumb for a while, making sure that no one else could see it. Then one Saturday when she was home alone, she began picking at it. She had been dreadfully hungry that day and the Little Nightmare was looking particularly candy-like. To her disappointment, she found that the covering was nothing but her own thick, hardened skin. The inside was hollow, save for the tiny carcasses of a few dead sink flies and a bright red seed. She planted the seed behind the house, but nothing grew from it.

***

Thamarai ended up making a number of mistakes with the record notebook. The first was to show it to S.T. Priya. She was not sure why she did this; at times she mistakenly felt like S. T. Priya was her friend and tried to share things with her. S.T. Priya glanced at the notebook and then gave Thamarai a deep, searching look which made her feel like sneezing. As she might have expected, S.T. Priya just saw the most generic sort of botany record notebook content and nothing else.

"You know who keeps dirty old record notebooks like this?" S.T. Priya said.

"Who?"

"You. You are a loose who collects dirty things."

"I don't know why I showed you this," said Thamarai wearily.

"Even I don't know," said S.T. Priya. "Imagine how it is for me. I'm just sitting here minding my business and then you come and show me something like this. *Boossssk* my life gone."

Thamarai decided any further questioning would be useless and tried to show the notebook to Prasanna.

"Is it the one you were supposed to throw away?" she asked.

"Yes. I keep forgetting to throw it out."

"It probably has insects in it. And insect eggs."

"Yes, it does."

"Do you want *me* to throw it out?"

"I just want you to look at it."

"I don't want to touch it though."

"I will touch it, you just read it."

"Okay. I'm covering my nose in case there are spores."

Thamarai turned the pages while Prasanna closely studied the diagrams and entries. She read slowly, and asked Thamarai to go back a few times so she could re-read something. Finally, Thamarai closed the book, and Prasanna took her handkerchief away from her nose.

"Well?" asked Thamarai.

"I don't understand. It's an ordinary botany record note."

"Really?"

"Yenna really, are you playing with me?"

"Nono, it seems like something else to me. That's why I'm asking."

"Like what else?"

"You didn't read anything strange?"

"What would be strange in a botany record notebook?"

"Like maybe you read about a paati."

"Whose paati?"

"Any paati."

"I didn't see anyone's paati in there."

It was also that time of year when the days began to feel like one, long, slow-moving day of oomai veyil. Every day was the same. Prasanna was almost always mood out. Unlike others, who would either pretend they were okay or pretend they were not okay, Prasanna would say exactly what she felt.

"My heart doesn't feel right," she told classmates who asked what was wrong. "At the end of the day, P. Yamuna is our classmate. This is happening to her and we can't do anything. Who are we to do anything? We are no one. That's why my heart just doesn't feel right."

She looked so utterly dejected that even teachers began

asking if she was okay. To them, too, she would say, "My heart doesn't feel right, miss. That's all." The teachers would tell her to eat more rice, drink Horlicks, sleep early, and go to the temple more regularly to clear her mind.

S.T. Priya could not understand why Prasanna was feeling so bad. If it had been anyone else, she would have dismissed it as putting scene. But with Prasanna, it was different.

"Is it me?" S.T. Priya asked Prasanna, when it all became too much for her. "Did I do something to upset you? Just tell me."

Prasanna put her arm around S.T. Priya's shoulders and explained how unfair it all was, how P. Yamuna was more to be pitied than anything else, how the English Sir should be skinned alive for what he was doing. But Prasanna also knew there was nothing to be done about it, because who were they after all?

S.T. Priya either saw something in what Prasanna was saying, or simply decided it was time to change sides. Whatever the reason was, from that day on, S.T. Priya stopped spreading rumours about P. Yamuna. The rumours still spread, but without S.T. Priya's fertile imagination, they became markedly less interesting.

Thamarai herself was more bothered by the idea that nothing could be done about the English Sir. All this would surely come back to him someday, but she wanted to be there to see it. So far, retribution seemed to be taking its own sweet time. He had recently received a commendation from a local social service group, and had bought a new motorcycle.

Thamarai began to think about her menstrual cycle. Like many people in the town, Thamarai believed there was something magical and uncontrollable about menstruation. It was a powerful thing. Her own menstrual irregularity was probably releasing all kinds of weird energy that was causing her to see supernatural things. Perhaps it could make her *do* supernatural things as well. Maybe she could do something about the English Sir. She decided she would study the record notebook more closely and see if anything presented itself. Something along the lines of piles, thought Thamarai. Piles would be good.

***

Name: Naatu Pepsi.
Danger Classification: Harmless, slightly annoying.
The Summoning: In the GGHSS, the very idea of Naatu Pepsi conjures up expectations of a cold sweetness cascading like a river down the throat, washing away the thick sourness of the day. It promises millions of small bubbles that bite, millions of beautiful people with their heads thrown back and the sun shining on their throats. Of all the GGHSS consumable items, Naatu Pepsi is one of the most expensive, which is why no girl can consume it solely on her own. In order to procure this drink, a round robin is held where everyone contributes anything from twenty-five paisa to five rupees. A suitably terrified younger girl is summoned from the 6th standard class and tasked with the errand of buying the Naatu Pepsi. She is sent with an empty water bottle, fifteen rupees, and the promise of dire consequences if she fails to return.
Composition: It must be noted that Naatu Pepsi is not Pepsi. It is in fact a generic and most likely spurious cola powder that is mixed in soda water and sold in small, roadside stalls.
Mode of Operation: When the bottle finally arrives, the terrified 6th standard girl is given a round of compliments, then sent on her way. The bottle is surreptitiously passed around, consumption being relegated to one small sip per person.

Naatu Pepsi can be an extremely insidious entity, depending on its mood. Once ingested, it slithers down into the body and immediately jams thick branches into muscle, cartilage, and bone. Once it has firmly embedded itself, the host will first become relaxed. A melancholic state will come over them, but the ensuing thoughts will be strangely comforting—so comforting that even after the state finally lifts, the host will sometimes try to re-create the feeling.

Naatu Pepsi can also cause excessive belching. Sometimes the belcher will bring up a substance that looks and feels like rubber cement.

***

A few days later, S.T. Priya reluctantly shared the news that the mysterious locked room in her house had somehow become unlocked.

"This morning we saw the lock was broken," said S.T. Priya. "No idea how it happened. Locks shouldn't break like that, even if they are rusted. But this one? Complete." S.T. Priya flattened her hand and moved it parallel to the ground, to show just how complete the lock break was. Thamarai was eager to learn more, but S.T. Priya would not elaborate. At maths tuition the next day, Thamarai saw that a new lock had already been placed on the door.

"Where is the old lock?" Thamarai asked.

S.T. Priya pointed to a thick, rusted lock lying on the ground. Its broken shackle had a jagged edge, as if someone had torn it open.

"You can still sell it for scrap," said Prasanna. "You will get a good price for a lock."

"I don't care what they do with it," said S.T. Priya. "I'm not touching it in any case."

"Why have you just thrown it on the ground like that?" asked Thamarai.

"Don't start all that now, why is the lock on the ground, why is the crow in the tree," snapped S.T. Priya.

"Tell what was in the room," said Thamarai.

"We didn't look in the room, okay? Now don't keep going on about it," said S.T. Priya. "I already told you everything."

"What if something was in the room though?"

"Like what?"

"Like… a paati."

"Whose paati?"

"Just a general one."

"Aiyyo! Just leave it now. I'm sorry I said anything."

"I told you that room was haunted," said Thamarai. "Otherwise, how will the lock just come off like that? It's haunted. By a paati."

"You've gone completely mental this time," said S.T. Priya with concern.

"That room is haunted."

"Your brain is haunted," S.T. Priya said.

At this point, S.T. Priya's father appeared and maths tuition began.

***

About a week later, Gopalan Sir disappeared. At least, Thamarai thought he had disappeared; everyone else seemed to believe he was unwell and resting at home. One morning, he did not appear for physics tuition. Instead, a terrified-looking young man was sent to inform them that Gopalan Sir was not well, but had sent a dummy exam paper. The girls were to complete the paper, then send their answers back via the terrified young man, who would wait for them to finish. Thamarai answered the questions with her usual enthusiastic tangle of formulae, numbers, chemical equations, and snippets of poetry. But the next day, when the young man brought back the corrected papers, Thamarai's answer sheet was marked 100% correct. At first, she thought it was a mistake. She showed the paper to Prasanna, hoping she would laugh.

"See," Prasanna said with a smile. "You can do well if you try. Congrats kanna, I'm very proud of you."

The same thing happened with every question paper the terrified young man brought. Thamarai would write whatever she felt like, and it would be returned marked 100%. Thamarai realized, with a certain degree of horror, that she was answering everything correctly, without even knowing it. At first, she thought that everyone had been marked 100% correct. She tried changing up her answers, and in one answer sheet, she was sure she had written a generic leave letter and nothing more.

Dear Sir/Madam,

As I am suffering from fever, I am unable to attend class for one day. Kindly request you to grant me leave for the same.

Thanking You.
Thamarai

This too came back marked 100%. Thamarai could see that it was a leave letter—or was it? Had it changed in some way? Or had she thought she was writing a leave letter when she was actually answering the questions? Now when the corrected papers were returned, girls would ask to study Thamarai's answers. S.T. Priya's usual barbs were now soaked in jealousy, which Thamarai found very annoying. Prasanna did not say much, but she kept smiling warmly, genuinely happy to see this shift in her friend.

"Go on," Thamarai said to S.T. Priya one day. "Ask me anything. Ask me the easiest physics question. I won't be able to answer, I'm telling you."

"Don't show off too much, okay?" said S.T. Priya. "You're a very big and esteemed physics scientist. Enough? Just taking my life."

Prasanna would not listen to her either, though she admitted that she was surprised to see Thamarai learn everything so quickly.

"I *haven't* learnt anything!" wailed Thamarai helplessly.

"Seri seri," said Prasanna.

"I don't know what I'm writing," said Thamarai. "I'm just writing nonsense. Even I know that."

No one would listen to her. She gained a reputation for being someone who claimed not to study but scored the highest marks anyway. Thamarai had never felt so frustrated in her life.

In the meantime, there was no news of Gopalan Sir. One day, when they asked the terrified young man what was happening, he avoided looking at the girls and said, "Don't worry, Gopalan Sir will come."

"Do you know when he will come?" asked Prasanna, always the boldest.

"He will come soon," said the young man, looking thoroughly uncomfortable. Then they all watched him cycle off furiously, like he couldn't get away fast enough.

***

Name: Flower Girls.
Danger Classification: Moderately Dangerous.
Description: GGHSS cataracts are exceedingly supernatural, affecting girls with perfect vision as soon

as they arrive inside the campus. The cataracts appear to contain flowers commonly found in Tamil Nadu: a girl may have shoeflowers, chilli hibiscus, tube rose, four o'clock flowers, crossandras, bougainvillea, golden shower flowers, and the butterfly pea all crowding for space inside her eye. Sometimes, the flowers obscure the iris entirely, causing the eye to resemble a riotous garden trapped in resin.

Mode of Operation: While such eyes are very beautiful to behold, they are excessively painful. The flowers insinuate themselves into the optic nerve, twisting forward until they have successfully penetrated the brain. From there, the flowers drain the girl's most recent memories, converting them into dark blue pearl-like objects which are then distributed throughout the body. Apart from this, the affected girl will gain the ability to share prophecies. Prophecies will always be delivered in threes: one being a true prediction of the future, one being a lie, and one being unverifiable. As a result, these prophecies are generally ignored. Due to the pain of the cataracts, these girls will spend most of their classes sitting and dreaming about brightly coloured things or historically important natural disasters. They will never do well in school, though they will be able to accurately describe what it was like when an infamous F5 tornado hit Kansas in the late 1950s.

***

On an otherwise ordinary afternoon, sometime after the quarterly exams, P. Yamuna came running into the classroom in tears. She was inconsolable, burying her face in her school bag and sobbing. Her benchmates crowded around her, trying to find out what was wrong, but she would say nothing.

It was S.T. Priya who told everyone. She had followed P. Yamuna into the classroom, and looked a little stunned. She had seen it all happen, she said. P. Yamuna was coming out of the English Sir's room as usual when the Botany Miss appeared and began to yell at her for wandering in the corridors. At least that's what she started to yell about; then she began yelling about all sorts of things.

"Don't you know how to behave properly? Don't you have any shame? The school is stinking with your goings-on. Don't you know how a student should behave? You're acting a bit too much nowadays and if you're not careful, you know what will happen. You know what happens to those kinds of girls. Because nothing will happen to anyone else. Just to you."

This marked the first time that an adult had said something.

For the rest of the day, P. Yamuna stayed in the classroom, rooted to her desk. Many girls went up to her to ask if she was okay, but she simply shook her head, unwilling to talk. Her face was red and puffy with tears. When the Zoology Miss came for class, she ordered P. Yamuna to go wash her face, drink some water, and then come back inside. P. Yamuna did as she was told. She stopped crying but was quiet for the rest of the day. It was almost like she wasn't there at all.

"Listen," S.T. Priya said to Thamarai. "I didn't do anything."

"When?"

"All those things I said before about P. Yamuna, I mean."

"You didn't say them?"

"What I mean is—"

"You did say them though."

"I'm not saying I didn't but—"

"You said them a lot. Every day you said."

"I know! Just—"

"Many times a day you said."

S.T. Priya threw her hands up and settled back with a scowl. Meanwhile, Prasanna went and sat beside P. Yamuna, talking to her softly, saying, *Past is past, you should focus on the future now, there's no reason why your future should be spoiled. Just do your work, or don't do it. That's up to you. Either way, just mind your business and keep your head down. If the English Sir talks to you, just keep saying yes sir. He will send you back quickly if you do not chat with him. At some point, he will move on to someone else.*

P. Yamuna just sat there. Perhaps she was listening; it was hard to tell. When the last bell rang, she quickly gathered her things and left.

"Well?" asked S.T. Priya when Prasanna returned to her seat.

"I don't know," said Prasanna. "Botany Miss really tore into her."

"She did. I saw," said S.T. Priya.

"Can only tell a person so much. After that it is up to them," said Prasanna, collecting her things.

"Did she say anything about me?" asked S.T. Priya, a little anxiously.

Prasanna frowned. "Why would she say anything about you?" she said.

"Because," said Thamarai, giving S.T. Priya a friendly tap on the shoulder, "she is the one who went around spreading rumours, making everything worse."

"My dear mother, can you just shut your mouth for a bit? Please?" said S.T. Priya, bowing her head towards Thamarai with folded hands.

"She didn't say anything about you," said Prasanna. "She was mostly just crying."

The three girls made their way down the corridor, then down the stairs. S.T. Priya kept talking about how she hadn't meant anything by the stories, that it was just some silly nonsense. Surely people had the sense to know that none of it was true. Prasanna said nothing, and when Thamarai tried to chime in, S.T. Priya told her to shut up. Thamarai fell behind them as they walked, unwilling to engage any further. Suddenly, she collided into both of them. They were standing still, staring.

A few feet away, in the open corridor, the girls saw P. Yamuna sobbing again. The English Sir was standing a short distance away from her, trying to look elsewhere as he spoke. Thamarai wondered what he was saying. Was he telling her not to worry, that he would have a word or two with the Botany Miss and no one would ever dare to yell at her again? Or was he telling her she was overreacting, that it was nothing? Whatever it was, it was making P. Yamuna so upset that her face had turned an alarming shade of red.

It was Prasanna who moved first. She walked to the cycle stand, across from where P. Yamuna and the English Sir were standing. The English Sir could clearly see Prasanna, and she was well within earshot. S.T. Priya followed her and stood behind her. Thamarai walked over too and stood next to

Prasanna, having absolutely no idea what was going on, but feeling she should also take part. They could hear P. Yamuna's ragged voice, tinged with sobs.

"Why won't you do anything?" she said. With tears rolling down her cheeks and her hands twisting her handkerchief, she looked very young. The English Sir looked impatient, like he wanted to leave.

"What do you mean?" he said. "Why should I do anything?"

"Do you know how she yelled at me? Everyone saw! Everyone thinks I'm—"

"For the last time, this is your problem. Why you have come crying to me about it, I don't know."

The English Sir turned to the three girls. "Go home," he called out. "Why are you loitering here? Go home now."

"We are waiting for P. Yamuna, sir," called out Prasanna. "My appa said we were all to come home together."

"She will join you later."

"Aiyyo, I'd rather not leave without her sir. Appa will get angry."

"Go wait for her somewhere else then."

They shuffled towards the gate, ensuring that the English Sir could still see them, and they could see him.

"Enough of this," said the English Sir to P. Yamuna. "They are waiting. Just go home."

P. Yamuna looked at him. She had stopped crying, but her eyes were swollen and red.

"Why are you doing this?" she asked quietly.

This seemed to anger the English Sir even more. "Don't bother me with such things again," he said and abruptly walked away.

P. Yamuna stood where she was for a few seconds. Thamarai wondered if she was planning to do something extreme. But she soon came and joined them. Silently pushing their mopeds and cycles, the four girls walked to the road. P. Yamuna walked in front of them, the setting sun shining out brightly behind her silhouette. She did not look lonely. She looked like she was already gone, like she had crossed over to a different place. They walked a little way along the road into town, then stopped at the junction. P. Yamuna turned to look at them.

"Okay," said Prasanna.

P. Yamuna nodded. Then Prasanna and S.T. Priya turned their mopeds around and revved them up. Thamarai turned her cycle, too, and clambered onto the seat. The three of them headed back down the road, towards their homes. After a moment, Thamarai looked back and saw that P. Yamuna was still standing there, watching them go. Almost like they were friends just saying good-bye, like this was a normal, everyday thing.

Thamarai waved at her and knocked down three small children who were cycling beside her.

***

Supernatural Entities and You

Hitherto, we have discussed the behaviour and lifestyles of some of the GGHSS supernatural entities when left to their own devices. But researchers must also ask what those same entities can do for those of us in the real world. It has been documented that some girls—those who are more attuned to the supernatural—have been able to see and even interact with certain entities, such as Sand Worms, Paatis, Little Nightmares and Sex Demons. Though these entities never engage willingly, researchers and archivists are encouraged to convince them not just to interact, but to work towards the betterment of our scientific community. These entities may hold the key to combating a number of social evils, such as poverty, belief in superstitions, and spitting in public.

Those interested in this exercise should note that, of all the entities, the Sex Demon is the least willing to interact with humans, but also the easiest to influence into interaction. We are interested to know how the aforementioned entity behaves in different situations. For example, how does the Sex Demon fare when set on fire? How does it respond when chased relentlessly around the school? Does it make its own clothes? We encourage the reader to explore other ways in which the supernatural entities at the GGHSS might be exploited to the entertainment and advantage of our country.

***

Soon after the incident with the Botany Miss, P. Yamuna resigned as class leader. None of the teachers objected. Her days changed markedly as she slipped into her new role as just another inconsequential girl. During assembly, she quietly stood in line, periodically dabbing at the sweat on her upper lip with her handkerchief. During the day, she stayed in the classroom, opting to eat her lunch at her bench. After school, she went straight home, not even looking up while cycling.

There were changes in her appearance too. In the GGHSS, two types of daavanis were allowed: a nylon one and a cotton one. The nylon ones were a bit more attractive, more transparent, easier to handle, and quicker to dry. The cotton ones were awkward, stiff, opaque, and less forgiving if they got a sweat stain on them. P. Yamuna made the change from nylon to cotton daavanis, and re-styled her hair with a centre parting, ensuring that any stray hair was firmly pinned down with multiple bobby pins. She also took to applying turmeric on her face on a regular basis, so she now had a permanent yellow hue about her. She seemed to be trying to suppress her beauty, to mute her allure as much as possible.

For the most part, she succeeded. Whatever spark of arrogance or youth she had was quenched, and she now went around with the characteristic slump in her shoulders, as if she was trying to hide inside herself.

Prasanna did not want to be class leader, but a number of teachers insisted she take the post. They knew that with Prasanna, there would be no rumours or inappropriate behaviour. Prasanna had absolutely no desire to interact with the English Sir more than she had to. She looked at his hairline when she spoke, stood a safe distance from him, and refused to engage in any verbal interaction beyond "Seri sir yes sir". Once, he had tried to call Prasanna to his room, but she had insisted on standing near the door, ensuring it was kept wide open, so she could leave as soon as possible.

One afternoon, Thamarai watched as a 10th standard class sat under the trees and wrote a mock exam. It occurred to her that the English Sir's next girl could be sitting there. Thamarai thought about how in some movies, the villain got his comeuppance by being beaten by his victims. The problem was that the women never seemed to hit the bad guy hard enough. He would yelp and shake and wince, but it always seemed comical. Seeing a man being beaten with brooms or by small women using weak fists was always funny. Thamarai didn't know why; it just was. The villain always looked laughably scared when he was being beaten about the head. Why was the punishment always so visually absurd? Was it a silly thing for a villain to be punished? Even if the hero beat a rapist, he never seemed to go at it 100%. Maybe it was because in the movies, the heroine didn't really matter.

We are no one, Thamarai thought to herself.

***

On Forced Interaction with Supernatural Entities

Many researchers believe it is absolutely essential to capture supernatural entities and keep them in captivity. We understand that this can be beneficial for research purposes, provided that you don't die in the process, that you don't abandon the entities afterwards, or try to keep them as pets. The following tips can be useful in ensuring that you and your supernatural subject get the most out of your time together.

1. The luring and seduction of a supernatural entity can often take a great deal of time and patience. Slow seduction is the best and most effective way to forge a bond with the supernatural, but researchers rarely ever have the patience for it. It can take years to gain the trust and friendship of a single Sand Worm or Paati, and even then one may not be successful. Despite being incredibly tedious, these efforts can result in some of the most informative and loving bonds between the supernatural and ourselves.

2. The use of cages, leather restraints, chains, and/or verbal threats is not altogether frowned upon. We are aware that when one is in a hurry, these are without a doubt

the best ways to capture and keep a supernatural entity for a certain period of time. Many have asked if these methods hurt supernatural entities, and the answer is absolutely, yes they do. It also makes the entities reticent, unwilling to part with information, and sulky.

3. The wrestling of supernatural entities into these bindings, verbal or material, can be a physically taxing process, so we recommend that our researchers engage in daily Swedish exercises for about a year before making an attempt. Practice ruthlessness, irrationality, and selfishness. Do not consider the supernatural entity to be capable of feeling or thought, although it totally is. Be mean to it for no reason at all. Promise to let it go if it cooperates and does what it is told. Never, ever let the entity go, no matter what.

4. Being firm supporters of eugenics and the caste system, we cannot in good conscience encourage fornication between the normal and paranormal, specifically between archivists/researchers and supernatural entities. The physical obstacles in this endeavour alone should be enough to put anyone off, but if perhaps it is the obstacles that are arousing you in the first place, consider questions of the future. Is this going to be a regular thing? Will you take the entity out for ice cream? What about children? What would they even look like? What if something happens to your genitals? We do ask that anyone considering this kind of fornication to please consider all these and more questions before taking any steps. We also ask that you discuss your intentions with our medical administrator.

***

Thamarai ended up neglecting the record notebook for a while because there were exciting developments at S.T. Priya's house. Several new locks had been put on the mystery room door, but they were always found broken the next morning. *Torn open* would perhaps be a more accurate description. After a few days of this, S.T. Priya's mother collected her daughters and went to their grandmother's house in town. S.T. Priya's father stayed in the house alone for a few days, possibly to demonstrate that there was nothing strange going on. But he too ended up shifting to the grandmother's place, stating that it was difficult to travel between the two homes. Thamarai now had to cycle to town first thing in the morning for maths tuition, then back for physics tuition, then to town again for school (she had long since given up going to chemistry tuition).

"I never liked that house anyway," said S.T. Priya. She was very happy staying at her grandmother's. Thamarai herself had been excited to see S.T. Priya's grandmother's house, but it was disappointingly ordinary and no one had given her any salted boiled peanuts.

"Something was always leaking or breaking," S.T. Priya continued. "So many cockroaches. Big lizards. Scorpions. I'm not going back there again."

This was in stark contrast to what she used to say about the house before the locks started breaking. S.T. Priya used to enjoy the cosiness of their two small rooms, especially during the rains, when everyone sat in the main room with the kerosene lamp on, reading old copies of *Kalki* while having vadai and ginger tea. She was fond of her little garden, where she grew nothing but shoeflowers and green chillies. She enjoyed watching the state government programming with her family every evening, sitting on the bedroom floor. Now S.T. Priya seemed to remember only the infestations, the accidents, and the strange birds that had visited the house. Thamarai was smart enough to not mention the haunted room or the paati again, though she really wanted to.

The paati had been on Thamarai's mind of late. She now knew that it was the kind of paati usually found inside the GGHSS. But how did a paati from the GGHSS get into S.T. Priya's house? And if it hadn't come from the GGHSS, then where had it come from? These questions weren't the only things on her mind. Thamarai was also thinking about revenge. She hadn't forgotten what the paati had done to her and wanted to get some payback if she could. If S.T. Priya's family were planning to move out, this might be her only chance.

One morning, Thamarai ditched maths and physics tuition

and headed to S.T. Priya's house. She was confident that the room would be open, since it seemed impossible to keep a lock on it now. If she was lucky, the paati would be inside. She had brought an assortment of things with her that she hoped could be used as weapons: safety pins, a bobby pin, a number of small rocks, a geometry compass. She wasn't totally sure how she was going to use these items; if worse came to worst, she thought she could throw them at the paati in quick succession.

Thamarai cycled down the road as usual and was soon standing in front of S.T. Priya's house. She almost didn't recognize it. Then she realized that she had never seen the house completely locked up before. A large padlock on the front door glinted in the morning sun. Some of the window shutters hung half open. On the ground, she saw about four other padlocks, all with their shackles torn apart. Thamarai walked onto the front veranda and easily pulled a couple of the shutters open. The inside room looked ordinary; there were scattered Tamil magazines, a towel left on the plastic chair, stacks of newspapers on the floor. The door to the mystery room was closed but unlocked.

She decided to make her way to the back of the house. There was the tap where she had tried to wash the old woman's stench from her mouth. Next to it was a washing stone, a line of dried clothes, a few broken plastic mugs, and a bar of blue soap on the windowsill. Everything looked commonplace and yet utterly strange and new. A broken red bucket lay abandoned in the yard, and a tiny scorpion walked across the criss-cross design on the washing stone. Thamarai recognized some of S.T. Priya's clothes on the line and an uncomfortable feeling washed over her. It was strange to see the clothes without S.T. Priya in them. She turned towards the house and saw the small, warped back door. If it was locked, she would leave. If it was open, she would go in.

Thamarai took a deep breath and pushed the door. It opened.

***

Name: 9D.
Danger Classification: Very dangerous.
Background: 9D continues to be one of the most mysterious and disturbing supernatural aspects of the GGHSS. The phenomenon manifests as a class full of

9th standard girls. However, it is worth noting that there is no 'D' section in this particular schooling system, so technically, 9D shouldn't exist. Research has shown that 9D is more likely to appear either on the Phantom First Floor or in empty classrooms at the outer reaches of the GGHSS buildings during the rainy season. However, there have been sightings at other times as well.

Description: On the surface, 9D looks harmless enough. It appears to be a class of young girls sitting on the floor, looking straight ahead. They are too well-behaved, deathly quiet and still. The longer one looks, however, the more malicious the class seems. One may first notice that the girls do not blink, breathe, or move, and all their faces are identical. After a few moments, the class turns en masse to stare back at the observer. If one continues to watch, one will see that the girls' faces are in the process of melting off and their mouths are jammed with rusty nails.

Mode of Operation: After turning en masse, the class begins to sing a song in high-pitched voices that causes terror to flood the observer's senses. Those who continue to watch 9D are eventually lured into the classroom. There is no information on what happens to these individuals afterwards. A general warning has been issued that if one stumbles upon 9D, one should refrain from looking at the class and leave the area immediately.

***

The inside of S.T. Priya's house smelled a little musty and a little like fried potatoes. Thamarai quietly made her way into the main room. She had seen it so often from the outside that she felt like she was walking onto the set of a Tamil serial on TV. However, there was only one thing she was really looking for.

She went to the door of the mysterious room, opened it, and stepped inside.

It looked like any other room. Dusty sacks were stacked against one wall. A broken chair stood in the middle of the room. Thamarai could see the tiny, frail skeletons of numerous lizards. There was a small pile of cockroach carcasses in one corner. Soft, grey dust lay thick on the floor, and above her head, black strings of cobwebs, built by long-dead spiders, hung down like decaying banners. There was one window on the far wall, completely covered in grime. There was no paati.

Thamarai felt her heart sink with disappointment. Everything seemed very commonplace and ordinary. Perhaps the room wasn't supernatural at all; perhaps it was just a room. Maybe the paati had disappeared. She turned, prepared to take a closer look at everything. And then she saw it.

She had thought it was just another dirty sack. But now, she could see that the dark grey thing in the corner was moving. Bony arms were crawling up the wall, very slowly, and a harsh voice was singing something Thamarai did not recognize. The voice was unnatural, like a chemical taste in a sweet. Thamarai watched as the thing inched its way up the wall, very, very slowly. Its song would become very loud, like a shriek, then die away so it was barely audible. Thamarai did not like any of it. Her previous ideas of revenge were quickly disappearing. She tried to edge away but the paati turned and faced her. It was the same face full of wrinkles. No eyes or nose, and just a gash for a mouth. Thamarai stared, wanting to run, but unable to.

She finally managed to turn and immediately felt something pounce onto her back. It was clawing at her, breathing in her ear. She tried to slam herself against a wall, but all the walls of the room seemed very far away. Everything seemed far away. She was stumbling around in the middle of nothing while the paati bit at her hair and dug her claws into her back. *What if she does it again,* Thamarai thought. Rage began to run through her arms, teeth, and fingers. It was the vomiting that really angered her. The more she thought of it, the angrier she got. To have something drag you by the mouth, then vomit into it—it was too much. She would not let it happen again. Thamarai threw her hands over her shoulders and felt them close around the scrawny neck of the paati. She yanked the paati forward, feeling skin rip from her back while the paati screeched in her ear.

She could see the paati's face clearly now. It looked like a grey, desolate landscape, dry and bereft of any life. The paati began to shriek and writhe. Thamarai tightened her grip around its neck. The paati was clawing at her face now. Before she could think about what she was doing, she gave a sharp twist with her hands. There was a dull crack and then the paati went still.

Thamarai stumbled outside and dropped the paati on the ground. It lay sizzling, on some patchy grass, now barely more than a crumpled collection of old cloth. It seemed to be dissolving in the dry sunlight. Thamarai stood over it, then slowly and deliberately brought her foot down on the head. She wanted to pull away and run, but she forced herself to press down, to grind her heel and toes into it. Even when the paati groaned and let out a high-pitched whine, she kept her foot down, watching intently to see what would happen.

It did not take long. The paati began to disintegrate, its skin sliding off like the peel of an overripe fruit. Soon there was nothing left but a grey mess of mucous.

***

Name: The Cycle Stand.
Danger Classification: Dangerous for 6th standard girls.
Description: The cycle stand is an area of dirt and sand located between the entrance of the GGHSS and the outdoor Noon Meal Scheme kitchen.
Mode of Operation: The cycle stand is an area of constant struggle. It is manned by two small, scared 6th standard girls, chosen for the task each morning by an indifferent PT Miss. On reaching the gates of the school, students must immediately dismount from their cycles, as it is forbidden to ride inside the school premises. The two 6th standard girls, who are constantly in the process of trying to muster up their courage, will do everything they possibly can to direct the girls as to where they should park. Here, the cyclist has a choice. She may listen to the 6th standard girls and have no further problems with her cycle. Or she may completely ignore them, walk right past, and park her cycle wherever she feels like. The 6th standard girls will watch this with marked dismay. Once the girl has left the cycle stand area, the 6th standard girls will now have to move the cycle to its proper place. This may often require both girls, because it is not an easy thing to carry a locked Hercules cycle.
Risk Factors: The 6th standard girls are at risk of two specific things. The first is cycle tangles. It is still a mystery as to how

these happen. The result, however, is that a snarl of cycles will become inextricably tangled with one another, usually at the handlebar and cycle chain areas (it is possible, but not yet proven, that the Chain Pisaasu has something to do with this). Untangling the cycles will inevitably lead to the loss of one or more 6th standard girls, who will be swallowed up by the snarl and never seen again.

The second issue is the crossing of the cycle stand itself. If a 6th standard girl wanders towards the boundary of the cycle stand area, she will find it next to impossible to find her way back again. Stories abound of small girls trying to retrieve a cycle that has been haphazardly parked near the boundary. Hopelessly, they push the cycle forward, never reaching their destination. It is unclear how many 6th standard girls have been lost in this way.

***

After the killing of the paati, Thamarai realized something had changed. She was seeing supernatural elements more clearly now, sometimes even clearer than the real world. There were some entities she recognized from the book, but there were many more that were new to her. For instance, the huge tree which stood near the cycle stand was infested with large spiders who periodically plucked up a 6th standard girl, only to drop her somewhere on the other side. The girl would always get up, bewildered, and the spiders would make a clicking sound like they were laughing. The hot, sandy assembly ground in particular was home to many different kinds of entities. Small, fanged cows ranged near the boundaries of the ground while the ghosts of missing akkas milled about with the other girls, pretending to be alive. Thamarai had even seen a group of Sex Demons, assiduously harvesting a tiny garden of millets.

Thamarai always tried her best to interact with whatever she saw. Her first ever interaction with a Sex Demon happened with one who was weeding a small, cultivated square of land. It was clearly not in any mood to talk, but as the notebook said, such entities were the easiest to force into conversation.

"You are the first supernatural entity I have ever spoken with," said Thamarai.

"We are not speaking." The Sex Demon had a nasal voice which Thamarai did not like. But she persevered.

"We are speaking. I am speaking to you right now," she said.

"I am busy."

"Busy doing what?"

"I am busy weeding and not talking to you."

"Why are you called a Sex Demon?"

"I don't know. Some idiot put that name."

"What's your real name then?"

"Mani."

"Hello, Mani."

"Hello."

The Flower Girls could not see Thamarai and did not interact with her. But Thamarai could see them: she enjoyed looking at the flowers imprisoned in their eyes, which were really quite beautiful.

Not all the supernatural phenomena were so harmless. The GGHSS had pockets of inertia tucked away in numerous places. If you stumbled into one of these, you were stuck until you could gather enough energy to kick yourself out. There were also more than a few poisonous and violent entities who attacked when Thamarai tried to say hello.

Change was happening with the sisters who lived next door to Thamarai. Nowadays, whenever she cycled home, she was met by them, nervously hovering near the thorn fence. The sisters had become extremely anxious about something, though it was unclear what it was. Nothing had changed in their routine, the VHS player was working fine, and there had been no lengthy breaks in the electricity during the day. But they both insisted that something was off. There was something wrong with the house, the furniture, even their parents. Everything felt like it had changed when the sisters weren't looking.

Something was happening in their dreams too; at the same time, every night, both of them would wake from the same dream. It was not a memorable dream—they were back at school for an exam, but they could not find their hall tickets. They always woke up just when the exam started.

Thamarai was not interested in hearing about their dream. She felt she had more important things to deal with. But the sisters would not let her go. They had no one else they could talk to, they said; talking to their parents was out of the question, and they had lost touch with all their old friends long ago.

"It's very upsetting," they said. "We have not gone for our walk for two days."

"Hmmm," said Thamarai sympathetically as she locked her cycle.

"We are constipated. We are getting white patches on our face."

Thamarai nodded, slowly backing away from them.

"What are you going to do?" asked the sisters.

Thamarai almost burst out laughing. "Me?" she asked.

"You must have some idea. Or maybe you can talk to Amma and explain."

"Explain what?"

"No need to talk to Appa. Nobody can talk to him."

"I don't understand what you want me to do," said Thamarai.

The sisters stared at her. They looked like small, scared birds, and Thamarai felt sorry for them.

"You should take some buttermilk," said Thamarai confidently. "Add some tulsi and pomegranate leaves and have an empty stomach in the morning. Avoid oil, salt, and sugar for next two weeks. I'm sure that will make a difference." Thamarai felt quite proud of what she had said—it almost sounded like a real cure for something.

The sisters looked suspiciously at her and then sighed. "No harm in trying I guess," they said.

"It will clear everything up," said Thamarai. "My aunt had the same thing."

The sisters seemed tired; they held each other by the arm, as if scared that the other might fly away. They did not even criticize Thamarai's appearance. She watched them walk back to their house, still holding on to each other.

***

Name: Ammani.
Danger Classification: Dangerous.
Description: Ammani is easily spotted by the fact that she is always in coloured dress. She wears a shiny candy

pink top with white trimming, a white midi with pink embroidery, and a crushed, white nylon dupatta pinned to her right shoulder. She always appears to have just washed her hair. Pink and white plastic bangles hang off her bony wrists. She even wears a pink and white pottu that she keeps worrying will fall off. Chunky silver anklets are wrapped around her large, dry feet and fake gold jimkis hang from her ears, almost obscuring them entirely. She breathes noisily through her mouth, making a signature raspy sound.

General Behaviour: Whenever someone notices Ammani, she tells them it is her birthday, which is why she is in coloured dress. She says that when she gets home, there will be a party. The walls will be lined with plastic chairs. Ammani herself will serve the chips, murukku, cake, and Rasna. Then everyone will play antaakshari.

Most girls are kind-hearted, and they let her go on, feigning amazement at all the wonderful things she talks about. She reminds many of them of a younger sister or cousin. Ammani will start to move closer. When the girls try to shift their attention to something else, Ammani will roughly turn their chin or stand right in front of them, and say things like "Why are you so black akka?", "Are you so arrogant because you think you are beautiful?", or "I think you are very stupid, isn't it?" Some girls will lose their patience and shove her aside or tell her to get lost. But they soon find that Ammani is stronger than she looks. She shoves, kicks, hits, and slaps with her mouth open, looking sleepy. She leaves bruises and has been known to bite. She scratches at eyes and tries to rip faces open. She empties book bags and breaks fountain pens, and the girls just watch, because there is nothing else they can do. On a number of occasions, she has sucked the blood out of a girl and eaten parts of her stomach. Thankfully, Ammani gets bored easily. Eventually, she will walk away, and the girls she has harassed will get up and leave as fast as they can, bloodied and bruised. It is not uncommon to come upon Ammani standing in a corner or at the head of the stairs, staring with her mouth open. If one does see her, it is best to ignore her and leave the area as quickly as possible.

***

The next few weeks were quiet. Prasanna was more silent than usual. P. Yamuna continued to keep her head down, spending most of her days drawing kolams in her notebook. S.T. Priya and her family were still at her grandmother's place.

"We had a break-in at the old house you know," said S.T. Priya. "Someone broke open the back door and came in."

"Oh really?" said Thamarai, feigning amazement.

The way S.T. Priya told it, robbers had torn down the back door and ransacked the house, spending a considerable time in the mystery room. Nothing had been stolen because, as S.T. Priya said, the robbers were cracks.

At physics tuition, Gopalan Sir had still not arrived. The terrified young man kept coming, giving a question paper to do, and taking back the answers. But many girls had lost patience with the arrangement. They were paying for tuition classes, not to do old exam papers over and over again—they could be doing that on their own, at home. One by one, girls stopped coming. Soon, the only girls left were Prasanna, S.T. Priya, Thamarai, and the girl who hosted the classes.

"Hey, I'm also going to cut," said S.T. Priya one day. "Why should I keep coming here like some idiot? That too I'm coming all the way from town."

True to her word, in a few days, S.T. Priya stopped coming. Thamarai could not figure out why Prasanna didn't stop too. She didn't need any kind of extra help, and yet here she was, wasting her time with a below-average maths teacher and a physics tuition with no teacher at all.

"I don't know what it is," said Prasanna. "I don't feel like doing anything."

"I never feel like doing anything," said Thamarai.

"You are right though," said Prasanna. "This is a waste of time. I should join some other physics tuition, probably in town."

"And maths. You don't need maths tuition either. Why unnecessarily spend money?"

"Maybe you are right."

One day, when the half-yearly exams were coming up, Thamarai found herself alone. Even the girl who hosted the tuition decided she would no longer attend classes. Thamarai was still allowed to sit at her dining table and do the exam papers, but she was asked to make other arrangements by the end of the month. Thamarai thought she should probably quit like everyone else, but for some reason, she didn't have the heart. Maybe it was because she was doing so well in her physics tests. She found that she felt sorry for Gopalan Sir. Apart from Prasanna, he was the only one who had ever believed that Thamarai could succeed. Now it felt like he had been abandoned by everyone.

After her final physics tuition class, she made her way over to the terrified young man who was waiting to collect her answer paper. She handed it to him and looked directly at his hairline.

"You need not come again. Everyone has quit tuition. Even I must quit now since there is no place to hold class," said Thamarai.

The young man fixed his eyes on her cycle.

"Okay," he said. "I will inform Sir."

"How is he? Is he doing better?"

"I actually don't know. I haven't seen him yet."

"Oh. Then?"

"The question papers come to me by post. And I send them back by post."

"That's strange, don't you think?"

"Yes, I suppose it is. I will take my leave now." It was not appropriate for a young man and woman to speak in public alone for too long. He quickly hopped onto his cycle and sped away.

Thamarai stood there, unsure of what to do. She was very curious about Gopalan Sir. She fondly thought of his slippery dentures, and how they always entertained her during class. Sending the question papers by post seemed exactly like something he would do, but it was still strange. Perhaps something terrible had happened to him, and the papers had been sent by someone else, so as not to arouse anyone's suspicion. Thamarai decided she liked this idea and mused on it in detail while she slowly cycled to school.

***

Name: Mouth.
Danger Classification: Harmless; inflicts negligible physical distress.
Appearance: This entity is one of the most unnerving in the entire GGHSS. It is impossible to know what it looks like because it is invisible, but one can get a rough idea of its size by feel and sound. As the name implies, Mouth is a mouth. Some have suggested that it is part of a much larger demonic entity. Even if this is the case, it is the only part of the entity that interacts with others. These interactions are of two distinct types.
Forms of Mouth: The most common interaction has been dubbed Moist Mouth. A girl, or sometimes a small group of girls, will become aware of the sound of moist and sticky lips opening and closing very slowly. This sound is usually heard directly over one's shoulder. The sound lingers, moving from left to right, and then directly in front of one's face. It gives the impression that something is about to appear, which is why girls affected by Mouth will often try and sit in crowded places to wait until the entity passes.

The second type of interaction has been named Soft Mouth. Soft Mouth operates on touch alone and can affect girls over a much longer period of time. While sitting in class or cross-legged on the floor of the open corridor, the affected girl will feel a soft and warm presence on her bare leg. For a while, the sensation may be felt up and down the leg until it finally grips the fleshy part of the calf or the thigh. The grip will be firm, but there will be no real pain. At this point, the Mouth is in the process of draining the water from the girl's body. The grip may move to the back of the neck, the upper arm, or the palm of the hand. It is usually dismissed as a stiffness, and the affected girl will not take this seriously until she finally faints from dehydration. When she wakes, she will have severe diarrhoea. At this stage, the girl will usually ingest copious amounts of water with equal amounts salt and sugar added to it. This will cause the Mouth to loosen its grip and fall away.

***

Sometimes there were good days. Thamarai would cycle smoothly and quickly and arrive at her destination without breaking a sweat. She would get to stand in the shade during morning assembly and Prasanna would spend the morning sitting next to her. There would be fried plantain in her lunch box. The afternoon light would be so beautiful that Thamarai would simply breathe it all in and smile. There were so many things that could turn an ordinary day into a good day.

This particular January day had started with a good morning, built of solid grey cloud that arched above the town, bringing the temperature down just a bit. It made a world of difference to everyone; the sea breeze was more refreshing than usual. The classroom was half empty, but the reason for this was unclear. Maybe it was an auspicious day, and some girls had stayed home to perform rituals. In any case, the general mood was improved.

After assembly, Prasanna had walked into the classroom a little bemused. She kept the chalk and duster on the teacher's table and went back to her seat.

"The attendance registers have gone missing," she said with a little chuckle.

"What, all of them?" asked Thamarai.

"All of them," said Prasanna. "It's the strangest thing. They are usually kept in the HM's room in a pile. Today, the whole pile is missing."

"Chee. Someone must have misplaced them," said S.T. Priya.

"We've checked," said Prasanna. "No sign of them at all. It's the strangest thing."

This situation was rendered even more bizarre when a slight, wiry girl came and informed Prasanna that some of the registers had been found again.

"You found ours?" asked Prasanna.

"No akka," said the small girl breathlessly. "They are being found all over."

"All over means?"

"No akka, all over means some were found in the assembly ground, and some in the cycle stand, and one was in the place they cook the noon meals akka."

"Don't lie."

"No akka, I was told to inform you so you can go and look for your register."

"I'm supposed to search the whole school grounds for our attendance register?" asked Prasanna, bewildered.

"No akka, yes you can take one other person with you they said akka."

"Me," said Thamarai, promptly standing up.

"But this is crazy," protested Prasanna.

"Yes akka, can't understand anything, thank you akka."

The slight, wiry girl stood on one leg, nervously fidgeting with her handkerchief. Out of pity, Prasanna let her go. Thamarai caught Prasanna by the arm and they set off... but Prasanna suddenly stopped.

"Should check the class first, no?"

She checked behind the locked bookcase and under it. She cast a sharp eye over the teacher's table and even over the first benchers. Once she was convinced that the ledger was not there, she and Thamarai set out to check other places.

The cycle stand was already buzzing with other class leaders, all looking for their respective attendance registers. One had found their ledger lying underneath a knot of tangled cycles. Prasanna and Thamarai searched the basketball court, the zoology and botany labs, and the assembly ground with no luck. They saw other class leaders who had found their attendance registers heading back to their classes. Prasanna frowned as she watched them.

"What is this, we seem to be the only ones who haven't found ours," she said.

"We will check upstairs," said Thamarai, grabbing her arm. She had spent almost the entire morning with Prasanna, walking beside her and feeling giddy. Thamarai did not want to give up the search just yet. The two girls walked to the staircase and made their way upstairs.

As they started up the third flight, Thamarai stopped and frowned.

"What?" asked Prasanna.

"Nothing, just... I think we are somewhere else."

"What do you mean?"

"I don't think we are where we think we are."

"Don't start with me now, come on," said Prasanna, walking ahead. Thamarai followed her slowly.

The Phantom First Floor looked the same as before, empty and abandoned. Dead trees stretched their branches into the open corridor, and in the distance, Thamarai thought she heard something like the sea. She saw one locked classroom shimmer, then disappear, leaving behind a pockmarked white wall.

"Okay," said Prasanna. "You look that side, I will look this side. Has to be here some place. Else they can give us a new register. This is ridiculous."

She watched Prasanna head to the wing on the right side of the floor. Thamarai made her way down to the left wing, thinking that she should have just stayed put at the stairs. As before, she passed classroom after classroom. At one doorway, however, she stopped short. An old, scrawny man was sitting at the teacher's table, surveying the empty room, as if waiting for something.

"Gopalan Sir!" exclaimed Thamarai, stepping into the room. She thought of calling Prasanna, but given the endlessness of the corridors, she was sure she was far away now. Thamarai was not worried; she knew that for Prasanna, everything appeared normal.

Gopalan Sir turned to her and smiled.

"Ah, at least one of you has come. Come, sit, we will get started," he said. His voice sounded the same, though a little tired. His eyes still burned with the disquieting brightness they always had. Thamarai hesitated to move forward. As glad as she was to see him, she did not want to attend a one-on-one physics class with Gopalan Sir in this supernatural part of the school. Anything could happen—what if the class kept going on and on, without end?

"Sorry," said Gopalan Sir. "My mind is all over the place today. What is your name?"

"Thamarai sir. How are you feeling now sir, feeling better?" she asked. Gopalan Sir frowned and stared at the table.

"Why do you ask that ma?" he said.

"You haven't been coming for tuition sir. For so many days you have just sent question papers for us to answer. I did so well in all of them. Everyone appreciated me."

Gopalan Sir was silent for a while.

"I... I couldn't come. Right?" He looked at her hopefully.

"Yes sir. So you sent question papers and I got 100% in all of them sir."

Gopalan Sir rubbed his face. He looked lost and confused, and it touched Thamarai deeply. The vigorous man who had thrown his arms about and entertained her with his slipping dentures now looked like any other old man.

"Another thing," he said, tapping the table. "I'm not sure how I got here."

"Cycle sir," said Thamarai. "That is how you usually get about. No?"

"Yes... only I don't remember..." He fell silent.

Thamarai watched him for a few seconds. She did not want to sit here all day. She decided that he would be okay if she left. There was no telling how long he had been here anyway. She would come back to check on him when she could.

She got up. "Okay sir. I will come and see you again sir," she said.

"Of course! See you soon," he said, seeming to regain some of his old spirit. Thamarai smiled. She made her way out of the room and down the corridor again. She had forgotten to check for the ledger, but she did not feel like going back. Anyway, she couldn't remember seeing any register anywhere.

***

Name: The Chain Pisaasu.

Danger Classification: Mostly harmless, causes mild physical distress.

Description: Commonly found in Hercules cycles, the Chain Pisaasu is usually invisible, though it has been known to show itself on cycle seats during the monsoons. In appearance, the Chain Pisaasu's body resembles a clutch of safety pins. Its mouth, situated on top of the safety pins, consists of multiple mandibles made of bone and plastic. It is generally found near the spokes of the back wheel, or on the chain itself. Its normal diet consists of petrol fumes and small pebbles, and its natural state is one of complete indifference to everything. However, for absolutely no reason at all, the Chain Pisaasu has been known to clamp down and tear at the hems of skirts, inskirts, chappals and ankles.

The damage that these entities can do is considerable. They consume copious amounts of cloth, human flesh, and bone. The Chain Pisaasu is also known to make the chain repeatedly slip when timid girls are trying to fix their cycles on a busy main road. Some researchers claim that leaving small piles of sand on the cycle seat as a peace offering can be an effective remedy, but this has yet to be proved.

Special Note: In 1984, a student by the name of S. Divya caught a Chain Pisaasu as it lounged on her cycle seat. Reports state that she kept the entity in her water bottle, where it lived for several months before dying of starvation. The body disappeared after a few days.

***

Thamarai was not sure how long she kept walking. She could have stopped and turned back at any time but for some reason she pushed on, peeking into empty classrooms. Finally, she decided she would head to class. She made her way to the stairs but could not find Prasanna; she had probably gone back to class already. Thamarai was about to continue down the corridor when she heard a faint buzzing sound, like a tubelight that had been turned on. She noticed a small room with a narrow door, nestled between two classrooms. The door was open. Inside, Thamarai could see that the room was crammed with small bookcases.

The GGHSS claimed to have libraries, but these were simply locked bookcases scattered about the main building, holding outdated brochures, dust, and multiple copies of a book called *Tension Koraipathu Yeppadi*. The bookcases in this small room, however, seemed to be unlocked. They were filled with foreign encyclopaedias, atlases, and English story books. Two small tables sat near the single window, with two wooden chairs. It was clean, cool, and quiet.

Thamarai could feel that there was something malevolent about this seemingly cosy and sweet room. She gingerly stretched her hand towards the entrance… and then stumbled back. The tips of her fingers were bleeding. She pulled out her handkerchief, wiped the blood from her hand, and then carefully tossed the handkerchief into the room. It was immediately cut to shreds in midair; some pieces floated farther into the room where they were shredded even more.

Thamarai stepped back. She gazed longingly at a set of atlases, wishing she could look through them. She liked seeing the different colours and terrains and using her finger to trace paths from one city to another. She sighed and made her way downstairs to class.

***

Name: The Library.

Danger Classification: Dangerous.

Description: The official library of the GGHSS is a truly remarkable space, filled with a collection of rare texts, research materials, and reference books that is second to none. Unlike other areas of the GGHSS, this area appears to be quaint and cosy, in that post-colonial kind of way which is alluring and safe for white people. There is a good chance that there would be no need for this compendium at all if it were only possible to peruse the tomes in this collection.

General Information: Some researchers have managed to collect information from unmanned aerial vehicles that have been sent into the library. Unfortunately, very little information can be gleaned from these machines before they are shattered to bits by the library atmosphere. From the meagre extant footage, one can see that the library contains multiple texts on the entities of the GGHSS, with one particular book appearing to be a complete compendium of every paranormal being that exists here. It is unclear why such a wondrous room of knowledge should be suffused with an atmosphere that rips absolutely everything to shreds. Little else has been gauged about this library, simply because it is too deadly to do so. For many researchers, the library is a Holy Grail which holds the key to most, if not all, their research and archival questions.

***

When Thamarai came back to class, she realized she had been gone for longer than she thought. Lunch appeared to be over, the attendance register was back on the teacher's table, and the class was already sunk deep into the sleepiness of afternoon. Prasanna was carefully writing out the answers to an old chemistry question paper while listening to S.T. Priya sing songs about sons betraying fathers. Thamarai sat down next to S.T. Priya and pulled out the botany record notebook. It occurred to her that the entry for the Phantom First Floor was missing some important information, which she could provide. She carefully wiped the nib of her fountain pen, tested it, and began to write.

Name: The Phantom First Floor.
Appearance: Looks just like the first floor except it is not the first floor.
Special Note on the Phantom First Floor: The Phantom First Floor is sometimes but not always located on the first floor of the GGHSS. Therein, it is possible to see various things, basically like desks, benches, thunderstorms, and other sundry items. Gopalan Sir can also be viewed there. A horrible library that will slice you to pieces is also available. Classrooms filled with frightening children should be avoided at all costs.

***

Despite having various doubts, Thamarai thought it was a pretty good write-up. The afternoon passed quietly and when school was over, Thamarai found herself leaving the cycle stand alone. Thamarai stopped to get air in her tires and then wended her way home, thinking about what she had seen that day. She was pedalling down the terrible road to her house when she suddenly stopped and stared.

The sisters' home was not something Thamarai would have normally noticed. It was not particularly interesting, and she disliked having to go inside it. When the sisters came to talk to her, Thamarai barely noticed the house behind them. Her attention was always taken up by the sisters themselves. But now it was impossible to miss that neither the house nor the sisters were there. They had completely vanished.

Thamarai was sure she had seen the house recently. Since every day was mostly the same, she had lost count of days and weeks. Had it been a while since she had heard from the sisters? The last time they had spoken, had they been sick? They had asked Thamarai to talk to someone for them. Or something like that. She wondered with a sinking feeling if their disappearance had been her fault. She got off her cycle and went over to the thorn fence to get a better look.

There was the usual plot, enclosed by layers of old thorn fences, the ground covered in dead leaves. There was the hand pump, the washing stone, and the old picture of Vinayakar in the corner, still adorned with a few dried flowers. But the house itself was missing.

Against her better judgment, Thamarai made her way into the sisters' yard, convinced that she was mistaken. Of course the house was still there; she just couldn't see it because of the bushes, or something like that. Maybe it had something to do with the sun.

She opened the front gate and stepped through gingerly. Scorpions and centipedes often lived under these leaves, and she had no desire to be bitten. She looked straight ahead to where the tiny box of a house should have been. But it wasn't. She took a few steps closer; it was definitely not there. She turned around and looked carefully at the rest of the yard. Then she turned back. Still, the house was not there. It was like someone had pulled it up and left the last row of bricks in place.

The family must have moved, thought Thamarai. But that still didn't explain what had happened to the house. There was no way they would have left without telling her. Seeing all four of them out in the sun, going somewhere—how could she miss something like that? She uncomfortably thought of the paati she had killed in S.T. Priya's house. What if this was payback for the paati, something that had to happen to maintain the balance between the real and the paranormal? The more she thought of it, the more supernatural the situation seemed. The family was, after all, considered to be "a little off"; everyone except Thamarai kept their distance from them, so not many others would notice their disappearance. But what could have done something like this? Thamarai imagined a legion of malevolent grey paatis descending on them, eating the family and the house to make up for their murdered compatriot. The more she thought about it, the more plausible it seemed.

The next day in school, Thamarai decided to ask around, to see if anyone knew anything.

"Who, those two loose sisters ah?" said S.T. Priya.

"Yes."

"Why would I know where they are?"

"I just—"

"They are not in the habit of informing me before they go anywhere."

"Okay, okay, but what about their house?"

"What about their house?"

"It's gone."

"Where has it gone?"

"That's what I'm asking you!"

"Why? Why are you asking me this?"

Thamarai winced and was about to turn away when S.T. Priya caught her hand.

"Wait, wait. You mean the HOUSE! Right?" said S.T. Priya.

"I've been saying the house this whole time," said Thamarai wearily.

"Well, why didn't you say so earlier?"

"Muruga!"

"Don't shout. You meant their house, correct?"

"Yes, yes, yes!"

"Oh! Yes, I know about the house."

"Well?"

"You want to see it?"

"You know where it is then."

"Sure. I have it here, in my kerchief, you want to see? Hey! Don't you want to see?"

Prasanna was a little more helpful in her answers, but for some reason she seemed impatient with Thamarai.

"You really don't know?" asked Prasanna, a little shortly.

"What do you mean?"

"The house was pulled down about a week ago. They were right next door to you, how could you not notice that? Where exactly is your head nowadays anyway?"

"And the sisters?"

"I don't know, staying with relations maybe? Gone to their grandparents' house? Probably staying somewhere else until the new house is built?"

"New house, ah?"

"Stop acting like this, it's annoying."

"Sorry."

"How can you not know about their house?"

"I don't know," said Thamarai honestly. She *should* have noticed. It must have been about a week ago that she spoke to them—something about a bad dream? Was it their mother that had been sick?

"I don't know where you are nowadays," muttered Prasanna.

"What do you mean? I'm here only."

"You don't act like it. Half the time you have your head in that book, doing God knows what."

"I'm reading it."

Prasanna rolled her eyes.

"See how well I did in physics tuition," said Thamarai, feeling she must change the subject.

"Hmm," said Prasanna, but she would not say anything more.

Thamarai was confused and unnerved by Prasanna's behaviour. She decided to sulk so that Prasanna would come over and ask what was wrong. But she did not come. Thamarai watched with mounting frustration as Prasanna spoke with other girls, studied, and then answered an old exam paper, until finally school was over. By this time, Thamarai was almost angry with her. She watched as Prasanna took a drink from her water bottle, then took out her moped key.

"Hey, what is it with you?" said Thamarai. "Why won't you talk to me properly?"

"I don't know da," said Prasanna looking straight at her. "You seem to be in your own world, and I don't think it is healthy. I am worried but I also know you won't listen to what I say."

"Who said I won't listen to what you say? Say and I will listen, promise."

"No, you won't."

"Yes, I will. Say."

"I want you to throw that old record notebook away."

"What? Why?"

"Because it's just an old botany record. It has botany diagrams and botany notes, that's it. There is nothing so special in it for you to keep looking at it like it's a sacred book. This is how people go crazy you know."

"Okay."

"Yenna okay."

"I will throw it out."

"Give it to me, I will throw it out."

"I said I would throw it out!"

"Do you know how many times you said you would throw it out? Still, you haven't."

"I will."

"No, *I* will."

"I will! I will do it today, promise."

Prasanna looked at her with genuine concern. "Seri," she said. "I have tuition in town today. I will see you tomorrow."

Thamarai felt a huge wave of relief as Prasanna smiled at her and touched her hand. Now that she had started writing in the notebook, she had no intention of throwing it out. But she would no longer look at it at school. Perhaps she would just leave it at home so there wouldn't be any risk of Prasanna seeing it.

Thamarai also resolved to pay more attention to what was happening around her. She was still uneasy about the fact that a whole house had been dismantled next door and she hadn't even noticed. She also did not like having Prasanna being short with her, so she decided she would spend a little more time and energy in being present. No matter what supernatural entity revealed itself, Thamarai would ignore it and try to be like everyone else.

But being present required a lot of energy. She found that she had to be aware and alert all the time, which was much harder than she thought it would be. It was easy for her to slip into slightly dazed states of mind where her surroundings faded and the layer of the world that existed under everything presented itself. The supernatural was becoming clearer to her, and her immediate surroundings were getting easier to ignore. Well, maybe not ignore—they just didn't matter as much as they used to. A door, a classmate, a house—they were all fading, just a little bit.

Mornings were relatively easy. There was no more physics tuition, and she was currently not going to maths tuition because she didn't feel like it. She could leisurely leave for school now, and she used the opportunity to try and be aware of the ride. She noticed that a new house was being constructed further down the terrible road. A young man who wore a blue shirt and blue pants followed her every day to school, keeping a fair distance but always there. When she reached school, he would stop, turn his cycle around, and head back the way he had come. This seemed like an awful waste of energy and time, and she wasn't sure how long it had been going on. But, Thamarai reasoned, this young man was a porikki, and that was just what porikkis did. Thamarai began to contemplate the life of a porikki, which she decided was okay to do because porikkis were a real-world thing. The life of a porikki involved following girls, sitting on walls and catcalling, sitting at the railway station and catcalling, and sitting at the temple and catcalling. It seemed like a dull way to pass the time and Thamarai wondered if this was something they *had* to do or just wanted to do. They would periodically be beaten by someone's uncle or brother, or the police. Thamarai had a feeling that these young men grew up to be the old men who were always at the bus stand, smoking beedis and staring into nothing.

There were other new developments on her way to school. A new temple had sprung up near the end of the bridge, and a little further on, Thamarai saw the Computer Centre. It used to be a sizeable tea stall, but now there were plastic windows, aluminium frames for the windows and door, and a young man wearing a tie and a lanyard. Rumour had it that there was also an air conditioner inside. The story was that this young man was a former porikki trying to correct his lifestyle. Thamarai sincerely wished him all the best.

She couldn't bring herself to leave the record notebook at home, so she let it stay tucked away in the back of her bag. At school, if she saw something odd, she resolutely turned the other way and tried to rationalize it. Sex Demons became gardeners. Paatis became ayahs. The Little Nightmares became abandoned wasps' nests. It unnerved her how easily the supernatural could be explained away as something ordinary.

The result of all these new austerity measures was that Thamarai became depressed. Sitting perfectly still while the other girls milled and moved around her was depressing. Eating the same lunch every day and listening to S.T. Priya's barbed comments was depressing. The young man who kept following her to school was depressing. In these dark times, Thamarai could not bring herself to open her school textbooks. Trying to study—it was asking too much.

The only thing holding her up during this time was Prasanna, but even her kind words were not as plentiful as they once were. Prasanna herself was falling into a kind of despondency. Part of it had to do with having to interact with the English Sir almost every day. But other things were bothering her too.

Once or twice, she had come over to Thamarai and said, "I understand what you keep saying da. What's the point in doing all this? After all we will just get married to some fellow, have children and die. Why do we need to study for that?"

While Thamarai agreed with the essence of this argument, she did not like hearing it from Prasanna.

"No, no," she said. "You mustn't think like that. You are destined for different things."

"Yenna different. At the end of the day, that's what happens to women, right?"

"Not all women—see Indira Gandhi. Or P. T. Usha. *You* can't be talking like this. It's making me very uncomfortable."

"Sorry da."

"It's okay. Don't lose your spirit like this. If you lose your spirit, what will the rest of us do?"

Without really noticing it, Thamarai soon started to read the record notebook again, whenever Prasanna stepped out to study in the corridor. In order to make it seem like she was doing something important and useful, Thamarai decided to add more entries to it. This time, she made tables and neatly labelled diagrams. She thought they looked very impressive. They would be ideal to use on her exam answer papers.

Every so often, S.T. Priya would have a peek at what Thamarai was doing.

"Crack," she said one day, when it was particularly oppressive and hot. She had been peevish all day.

"You only," said Thamarai.

"Listen, you keep all this up and we will have to report you to the medical authorities."

"Report yourself."

"Chee. Stupid."

"Nee thaan stupid. Un family full stupid."

S.T. Priya rolled her eyes and began rummaging through Thamarai's bag. She pulled out the botany record notebook and began to thumb through it. This time, it was giving off a dusty, sour smell like old, dirty clothing.

"Tell her to first get rid of this," said S.T. Priya, to no one in particular. "She won't improve as long as she is allowed to carry this garbage along with her."

Thamarai watched with wide eyes as S.T. Priya put the record notebook in her own school bag. A few benches away, Prasanna was sitting with some other girls, studying some chemistry problems.

"Tell her that I am going to get rid of this myself," said S.T. Priya, again to nobody in particular. "I don't know why, since she insulted my whole family and didn't even say sorry—"

"I'm sorry!"

"Too late. Damage is done."

Thamarai felt a small twinge of worry. If Prasanna saw S.T. Priya waving the notebook around now, she wasn't sure what would happen. Something bad probably.

"Give it," said Thamarai. She would not physically go after it. She did not want to draw more attention to it. S.T. Priya was now singing a string of her favourite Ramarajan songs while drumming along on the notebook.

"Give it," repeated Thamarai, a little louder now but still calmly. S.T. Priya stopped singing.

"And if I don't?"

"Just give it."

"Oho. Now you're threatening me."

"When did I threaten you? Just give it back, you don't want to be touching that."

"Why?" asked S.T. Priya suspiciously.

"Because there are millipedes in it." Thamarai had not really thought this through. She only said millipedes because she knew that S.T. Priya was scared of them.

"How can millipedes be in a book?" said S.T. Priya, somewhat less buoyant than before.

"They are in the binding. If you want, you can see."

S.T. Priya stared at Thamarai with suspicion. Then slowly, she handed the notebook back.

"Trust you to be carrying millipedes around with you," said S.T. Priya, her mouth pursed in disgust.

"I'm getting rid of it," said Thamarai, carefully hiding it at the very back of her bag.

Later that afternoon, Thamarai asked S.T. Priya to sing the entire songbook from the movie *Chinna Thambi*. She began immediately, and the afternoon passed peacefully enough.

***

Name: Palli Mittai.

Danger Classification: Harmless.

Description: There are many kinds of mittai or candy that circulate among the GGHSS. Horlicks mittai, kamarakattu, theyn mittai, cheeni mittai, orange candy, and Mango Bite are common candies that can be found in most of the small shops near the school. For some girls, the most fascinating mittai of them all is the palli mittai. The name refers to the fact that these tiny candies are the size and shape of lizard droppings, which is disgusting. Each piece is a little bigger than a grain of rice and contains exactly one cumin seed, covered in a hard coating of coloured sugar; blue, white, pink, green, orange, or yellow.

Mode of Operation: Most girls simply consume palli mittai without thinking, because they are small and cheap and ultimately there is nothing to really think about when eating them. But on consuming one, some girls' minds will explode with a myriad of questions. Specifically, how do they get that single cumin seed into the candy? And how is each one a different colour? Are they coated individually? As in, are people sitting in some room coating each cumin seed, one by one? The answer to how palli mittai are made may well be a logical and obvious one. But the mystery of this candy, and how that single cumin seed gets into every piece of candy, will rankle in these girls' heads for the rest of their lives. Even when they are older, they will wonder about it, and people will dismiss this as a cute quirk.

***

Nobody in town liked unseasonal rain. It was blamed for everything, from colds to stomach aches to earaches. The first Aani maasam rain in particular was considered to be unhealthy, responsible for the spread of flus, fevers, and headaches. Auto drivers who had no problem standing in the sun on a sweltering afternoon would refuse to take their autos out for fear of catching cold. The cycle ride to school was wet, cold, and miserable, made markedly more dangerous by the flooded roads and the numerous potholes filled with water. Girls learned the complicated skill of cycling through these roads while holding an umbrella. School during the rainy season was spent always being a little damp and cold while sitting on wet concrete floors. Teachers rarely showed up. Those who did would ask the girls why they had come to school when it was raining. The girls never had an answer.

On a Monday morning, when it was too late to stay at home, Thamarai was caught by a rainstorm halfway to school. She slowly came to a stop at the side of the road and waited. If it stopped, she would continue on her way. If it did not, she would head back home. Then she remembered that the electricity was always shut off during the rains. Sitting in the dark house with no power, swatting mosquitoes, seemed like too much despair to handle on a Monday morning. No, she would go to school, and hope they would not send everyone home. Sitting in class surrounded by a few girls seemed like a more pleasant way to spend the day.

Surprisingly, when Thamarai reached the 11A classroom, she saw that it was almost full. It seemed that everyone had made the same decision. The tubelight in the classroom was working and gave everything a cozy feel. Thamarai noted with a great deal of happiness that Prasanna was there.

"I thought for sure you would stay at home," said Prasanna with a smile when she noticed Thamarai.

"Staying at home is so boring," said S.T. Priya, as if Prasanna had spoken to her. "Better to be here. Anyway, there will be ginger tea and masala vada for tiffin later at my grandmother's house."

Rain meant no assembly, so the girls settled down to whatever they planned to do for the next few hours. Prasanna began another round of revisions for all subjects while S.T. Priya pulled out an old songbook and began singing off-key about milk, fruit, and gentle breezes. Thamarai listened to her and began to draw diagrams in her rough notebook. She drew a transection of Smiling Face, though she had no idea what could be inside. Perhaps there was a kind of hostel for young girls, a nice hostel, with all modern conveniences. Though she had never seen her before, she drew a diagram of Ammani—an unflattering portrait, with wasps inside her. Then she drew a few diagrams of herself—her own brain, her lungs, her mouth. The transection of her brain showed that it was in fact some kind of aquarium filled with bright, colourful fish and insects. In the transection of her lungs, she drew a sky full of kites, each one trying to strangle and pull down the others. When she drew the transection of her mouth, she replaced her teeth with flowers and drew a bed of colourful stones under her tongue.

Thamarai was wondering what to draw next when word came that the Chemistry Miss was on her way. The class half-heartedly pulled out their textbooks and waited for the teacher to arrive. Thamarai was putting the record notebook away when it slipped and landed on the floor. She immediately dived down to grab it, not wanting Prasanna to see. Thamarai was about to get back up when S.T. Priya put her hand on her head and shoved her down again.

"You can't get up now," whispered S.T. Priya.

"What?"

"I said you can't get up now."

"Why?"

"Because there's nowhere for you to sit."

"My seat is right there! Beside you!"

"Yes, but I don't want to sit beside you right now. You stay there."

Thamarai was taken aback. She had not expected S.T. Priya to imprison her under the desk during Chemistry class, and yet it seemed exactly the kind of thing she would do. Thamarai tried getting up a few more times and each time S.T. Priya sharply shoved her down.

"You stay there," she repeated firmly.

From under the table, Thamarai could see the teacher's sari gently swish against the ground as she took class. The Chemistry Miss—a thin, old woman who always looked like she was on the verge of fainting—was one of those teachers who focused solely on the first-bench girls and no one else. If the rest of the class was quiet enough, they could do what they liked. If they weren't quiet, the Chemistry Miss would throw things at the offenders with alarming accuracy. If Thamarai tried to get up now, she would probably get in trouble, so she decided to stay where she was.

Despite the fact that it was a rainy day and the floor was a little damp, she found it comfortably warm under the bench. The legs of the tables and benches surrounded her like a forest. She could see an array of feet, all adorned with silver anklets of varying ornamentation. Some girls wore ten rupee chappals and some had Bata slippers that cost Rs. 49.99. Some feet were still but many of them were shaking incessantly, tapping or moving from side to side.

Thamarai turned around, caught a glimpse of the expanse of benches that stretched behind her, and frowned. Everything looked too crowded. She noticed a thick mist floating near the ground, curling around the girls' feet. Something was not right.

"Here," Thamarai hissed at S.T. Priya, "Enough. Let me back up."

"No."

"There's something underneath the desk."

"Is it a pig?"

"What do you mean, is it a pig?"

"Remember when we were in 9th standard and we were sitting outside and that pig charged us? Is it like that?"

"No."

"Then who cares."

Thamarai noticed that the mist had curled up to her knees. The forest around her had now grown so thick that she could not see the other side of the classroom. The air was still, sweet, and oppressive.

She heard a raspy sound. Through the crowded bench and table legs, she caught glimpses of pink and white.

Thamarai quickly realized that this was Ammani. She was somewhere in the classroom. Thamarai did not want to encounter her. The thought of having her stomach devoured during chemistry class did not appeal to her. Ammani was one of the entities that frightened Thamarai the most. There was something about the sleepy, open-mouthed way she was said to assault girls that made her incredibly disturbing.

"You let me up right now or I will—" said Thamarai.

"What will you do? I'll hit you with my chappal. Stupid," said S.T. Priya.

The telltale breathing noise was getting closer. Another flash of pink and white. Then, Ammani was there in front of her, noisily breathing through her mouth while she wheezed the word 'akka'.

Thamarai scrambled up the bench and S.T. Priya shoved her down, keeping her hand firmly on her head. Thamarai tried her best not to look at Ammani. This was not easy because by now, the entity was right in her face. Thamarai could see that her eyes were completely black and small flies buzzed in and out of her ears.

"Akka..." wheezed Ammani again. Thamarai thought her best option would be to turn and try to crawl away. But there were too many human and wooden legs in her way; she could barely move.

"Akka..."

Thamarai covered her face with her hands and put her head

down. The notebook had said that if she did not acknowledge Ammani in any way, the entity would eventually leave. But this time, it seemed, Ammani was in no mood to talk about her impending birthday party. She prodded at Thamarai, pinching her arms and pulling her hair. Thamarai still didn't move. Ammani's assault became more violent. She punched Thamarai's head and arms. She kicked and slapped.

When Thamarai thought she couldn't take it anymore, she felt something sharp clamp down on her throat. With her eyes tightly shut, she flung her arms out, fingers curled. She was going to grab whatever came in her way; even if it pulled her fingernails out, she would hang on, claw and fight until Ammani let go.

She grabbed a handful of Ammani's face. Her thumb sank into something soft and she immediately squeezed her fist shut. She heard a screech as Ammani let go of her throat.

Then nothing.

Thamarai gingerly opened her eyes and saw that everything looked normal again. Ammani had disappeared and so had the mist. She could see the other side of the classroom, and the feet of the Chemistry Miss as she walked out after class was over. She got up; S.T. Priya was chatting with Prasanna and made space for Thamarai to settle back into her seat. The classroom buzzed with chatter and quiet laughter, but she just sat there, staring into nothing. Her heart was pounding.

She opened her clenched fist and saw it; void black, hard and round, strangely free of any blood or torn nerves. Thamarai had pulled out one of Ammani's eyes.

***

Name: Hero Penn.
Danger Classification: Dangerous.
Description: Despite the advent of the modern ballpoint pen, the girls of the GGHSS only write with a Hero pen. Available in maroon, green, and black, these fountain pens are workhorses. They are cleaned regularly and kept safely. Still, a number of pens manage to go missing every year and are never found again. This is because they are immediately absorbed by the Hero Penn.

On first glance, this entity will look like any other 10th standard student. It is only on closer examination that one sees what makes it so dangerous. The Hero Penn does not have fingers or teeth. Its fingers are a collection of fountain pens that have been jammed haphazardly into the stump of its arm with the nibs facing out. A large number of nibs can be found in its mouth, some in the place of teeth and some simply stuck into the gums at awkward angles. Standard blue ink drips from its mouth and eyes.

Mode of Operation: The Hero Penn is notorious for stabbing or biting unsuspecting girls and injecting them with ink. At some point, the girl will begin to wash away, like ink on a wet piece of paper. Fortunately, the Hero Penn can be distracted by more fountain pens, during which time the girls may make a speedy retreat.

***

Thamarai kept Ammani's eye with her at all times, wrapping it up carefully in a corner of her kerchief. She was sure it was special in some way, but she could not figure out how. As an object, it was not very remarkable. There was a slight give to it when Thamarai pressed down on it hard. It had no particular smell and the one time Thamarai had licked it, it had been like licking a marble. When Thamarai held the eye up to her own eye, however, she could see things. Sometimes she saw burning landscapes throwing twisty flames into a clear, blue sky, a forest of solemn fingers curling in the cold, a doomsday derecho showering down sharp diamonds on beautiful, intimidating Albertan farmland. The eye did not seem capable of doing anything else; still, holding it made Thamarai feel powerful. She was worried about running into Ammani again, but she seemed to have disappeared for the time being. Nobody else had seen a girl in coloured dress anxious to tell them about her birthday, either.

Meanwhile, a new kind of energy was beginning to reverberate through 11A. One of the larger tuition centres in town had set and printed out multiple 12th standard dummy question papers. These were now being passed around. The class had become quite caught up in these papers and was very keen to answer them all. There were two groups; the girls who were copying out the question papers by hand to answer later, and those who were directly answering each paper as it came to them. Thamarai was surprised by how many girls were actively involved in doing these dummy tests. She was even more surprised by the number of girls who seemed to have actually been studying all this time. Even P. Yamuna, who generally did not even open her textbooks, was now copying out the questions and clearing her doubts with the more academically inclined students.

Despite the reputation she had acquired with her physics tuition answers, when Thamarai said she hadn't studied, she meant it. She was as bewildered as ever by her textbooks. A sense of loneliness came over her as she wondered if she was the only one who truly did not know anything. Even S.T. Priya seemed to have covered a fair amount of maths, chemistry, and physics and was also tackling the question papers. The only person who seemed relaxed was Prasanna. After spending most of the year in studying and revising, she was taking it a little easy now. She did not try to coax Thamarai into studying.

Apart from all this, Thamarai realized that her aptitude for physics seemed to have disappeared. She was back to answering questions with rubbish that actually read like rubbish.

"Good that Gopalan Sir isn't here to see this, especially now," said Prasanna looking over one of Thamarai's answer papers.

"Means?" said Thamarai.

"Don't you know? He is very sick. He's been sick for a while now, full bed rest."

Thamarai thought of her meeting with Gopalan Sir on the Phantom First Floor. It was often said that elderly people who took a long time to die were waiting to finish something before they passed on. Perhaps Gopalan Sir had something to do here, though Thamarai couldn't think what it might be. She decided if she ever got to the Phantom First Floor again, she would ask him.

She wished she could get back there, just to get away from all the studying, but she wasn't sure how. The last time she had tried, the stairs had deposited her on the real first floor.

She thought that she might have more luck if she ran up and down in quick succession. Perhaps that would trip something up supernaturally? She tried it as often as she could, but still she always ended up on the normal first floor. She got so absorbed in these attempts that the PT Miss caught her and told her that if she saw her doing it again, she would break her teeth.

Thamarai began to feel frustrated. Study holidays loomed ahead and every day, Thamarai sat despondently in class wishing she was dead. One day, when she was feeling particularly restless, she decided to go to the school stores and buy all the sugar jellies she could afford. She carried them in a paper roll and began to circle the staircase, looking for an opportune moment to try her luck again.

She ran up the stairs twice, but both times, she wound up on the normal first floor. As she began her third attempt, the English Sir appeared and asked what she was doing.

"Why aren't you in class?" he said. He was slowly looking Thamarai up and down. She just stood there; something churned in the bottom of her stomach, but she knew the best thing to do was to simply stand still.

"What's that?" he asked, gesturing towards the paper roll of sugar jellies. Thamarai was holding them at her shoulder, like she was scared he would take them away.

"Nothing sir," said Thamarai mechanically.

"This is what I don't like," said the English Sir softly. "Just admit it. You have something there. Probably something you shouldn't have."

"Nothing like that," said Thamarai. She took a step back and noticed with unease that the corridor seemed to be empty. They were the only two people there. Thamarai wished she had never left the classroom.

"So. Let's see it," said the English Sir, folding his arms.

Give it to him, Thamarai said to herself.

She didn't have the chance. Before she knew what was happening, the English Sir had reached out his arm. She watched in mute horror as his fingers dragged slowly across her upper chest, then clasped around the paper roll of sugar jellies. Thamarai felt a rush of nausea run through her. She stumbled back and the English Sir smiled.

"Sugar jellies," he said. "You like them?"

She couldn't speak. Her stomach felt like it had fallen out of her body. She wanted to scream. She watched him put one of the sweets in his mouth and smirk at her. He handed the paper roll back.

"Get back to class," he said.

Thamarai turned, trying not to run. She could feel his gaze on her back. He hadn't actually done that, had he? Surely he wouldn't have. Thamarai must have imagined it. She replayed the incident and kept feeling his fingers on her chest.

When she finally reached her classroom, she gave the roll of sugar jellies to S.T. Priya, and put her head down, saying she had a headache.

***

Once when Thamarai was in 10th, she was cycling down an empty road near her house when a young man swerved towards her and grabbed her breast. She had watched helplessly as he quickly cycled away. A neighbour akka, who had seen it happen, immediately called to her and insisted she come into her house and have a glass of water.

"Listen," the akka said. "Now don't keep thinking about what happened. What's done is done. Just forget it. If you keep thinking about it, you will go mad. Anyway, what can you do? Nothing. So forget it." The akka advised Thamarai to go home and then go to the temple in the evening, to help ease her mind.

For the rest of that day, Thamarai tried not think of what the young man had done—and yet she kept thinking about it. She imagined grabbing his hand and pulling him off his cycle, dragging him along on the gravel road. She imagined swerving quickly so he ended up only grabbing a handful of air.

A few days after the incident with the English Sir, she was still forcing herself not to think about it. But no matter what she did, she kept remembering how he had grabbed the paper roll of candy, and how awful his fingers had felt on her chest. She felt herself fall into a pit of weary anger and helplessness. She looked across the classroom and saw P. Yamuna, sitting alone. Her stiff cotton daavani was demurely tucked in at all the required places. Her face looked jaundiced from repeated turmeric applications, and she was wearing the ugliest pair of glasses Thamarai had ever seen. It was almost as if it had been another girl who had been caught by the English Sir.

Thamarai realized that P. Yamuna had stood up and was now making her way towards her.

"What happened?" said P. Yamuna. "You're dull today."

"Nothing," said Thamarai, slightly surprised. "Are you well?" She was unsure of what else to say.

"Of course I'm well. Why wouldn't I be?" said P. Yamuna.

"I know things have been bit difficult for you."

"They have?"

"You know, with English Sir... and Botany Miss yelling."

"Oh."

"Yes. Shall I tell you something?"

"Not necessary."

"What?"

"I'm saying you don't have to tell me anything. Simply I came to sit here."

"You don't understand," began Thamarai.

"That's okay, I don't need to understand anything."

"I'm just saying that the English Sir will get his punishment one day. Maybe not the Botany Miss, because you kind of deserved what she said to you. But the English Sir definitely. One day he will get what is coming to him one hundred-fold. Fate won't leave a man like that. You just wait and see."

P. Yamuna stared at her. Then she suddenly chuckled.

"Someone keeps putting sugar in the petrol tank of his bike," she said.

"What? Who?" gasped Thamarai.

"Must be some town boys."

Thamarai hadn't expected this. She felt a strange sense of elation and justice. The idea that someone else could do something to the English Sir had never occurred to her. And of course, where girls could do nothing, boys could do something. Perhaps there were legions of P. Yamuna's cousin-brothers, uncles, and own-brothers all making secret plans to sabotage the life of the man who had misbehaved with their sister. This was completely plausible. This was probably what was happening.

Thamarai wondered what other things they might be doing to the English Sir. Someone could put garbage in his yard or steal his milk in the morning. They could dump cockroaches in his house. There were so many options.

"I didn't know about the sugar in the tank," said Thamarai. "Or the garbage in the yard."

"What garbage in the yard?" asked P. Yamuna.

"Someone has been dumping garbage in his yard," said Thamarai. She wasn't sure why she said it, except that it sounded like something that could probably be true. She decided that *made* it true in some way. And if it was making Thamarai feel a little better just by saying it, imagine how happy others would feel to hear it.

"The morning milk keeps getting stolen also," said Thamarai.

The more scenarios she thought of, the more she could picture them actually happening. In her mind, the English Sir was already getting some sort of payback, and it was giving her a certain relief.

"Hmmm," said P. Yamuna. Then she got up and left.

Later that day, Thamarai told S.T. Priya and Prasanna that the English Sir was getting continuously harassed. Someone was putting sugar in his petrol tank and throwing rocks at his door in the middle of the night. She enjoyed adding more and more to the story, especially since Prasanna's face brightened as she listened.

"Who is doing all this?" asked Prasanna.

"Town boys," said Thamarai. "One of them is related to our Yamuna, you see."

Prasanna grinned. "See? Our town boys are vera level. At least they can do something."

"You're lying aren't you?" said S.T. Priya, looking thoughtfully at Thamarai.

"Why should I lie about this?" said Thamarai.

"To cheer this one up, that's why," said S.T. Priya, putting her arm around Prasanna's shoulders.

"Chee, she won't do all that. Right?" said Prasanna.

"Yeah, why should I do all that? As if I have nothing better to do."

The news seemed to change Prasanna's mood. She regained a good deal of her old spark and even began teasing Thamarai from time to time. This, along with other distractions, eventually helped to dull Thamarai's memory of what had happened.

Thamarai was tempted to tell Prasanna about her own encounter with the English Sir. She wondered if it would make her feel better. Or perhaps Prasanna could help her, though she wasn't sure how. But Prasanna seemed so light-hearted and happy that Thamarai decided to keep it to herself.

***

The final chapter in the saga of S.T. Priya's old home happened a few days later; S.T. Priya's family officially vacated the place and were now going to rent a small house in town, near the grandmother's. The old house would not be given out for rent. Instead, the landlord decided he would extend the ground floor and build a first floor, so the building could accommodate four tenants instead of one.

"Who will pay to stay in that house?" said S.T. Priya. "Idiot house. No one with sense will stay in that house."

"You and your family stayed there," said Thamarai, and as a result, she was accused of maligning S.T. Priya and her family. But this drama ended quickly, as S.T. Priya had an interesting story to share about the house.

"I'm not telling you though," said S.T. Priya to Thamarai.

"Okay."

"See? She won't even say thank-you. Say thank-you."

"For what?"

"For telling you. Because I *am* going to tell you."

"I don't know what we are talking about actually."

S.T. Priya scowled and turned away. The truth was that no one, barring Thamarai, was interested in hearing about S.T. Priya's old house. Once the turbulence of S.T. Priya's feelings had settled, she told Thamarai the whole story.

"Do you know who used to live in my old house? Gopalan Sir. He lived there just after he was married. And you know where he was working at that time? Here. In our school. Teaching physics," said S.T. Priya, rounding out the story with a lyric from a film song: *"Va vaathiyaru ootanda, nee varaangati naan udamaaten."*

S.T. Priya looked at Thamarai with a subtle look of triumph.

"Is that all?" asked Thamarai.

"Why, what more do you want?" said S.T. Priya.

"It's not a very good story," said Thamarai.

"Look at this one, you tell her anything and she immediately wants you to include a fight scene and two duet songs. Get lost."

Thamarai thought about what S.T. Priya had just told her. She wondered if it might explain why Gopalan Sir was floating around the GGHSS. Perhaps he had some supernatural attachment to the old house as well. Thamarai decided that she would ask him that, too, if she ever got to see him again.

All around her, Thamarai's classmates were answering the dummy question papers, exchanging their answer sheets and laughing at their silly mistakes. Even Prasanna, who was already well-prepared, was doing a maths question paper. Thamarai thought about how odd it was that while she could never remember anything pertaining to her studies, she could remember perfectly the descriptions of most supernatural entities. She could even write about each entity in some detail.

One afternoon, she began re-working the Phantom First Floor entry. Her initial notes soon grew to an impressive paper several pages long, filled with diagrams, charts, and extra footnotes. She was rather proud of it.

As the others finished their dummy question papers, Thamarai wrote entries for a few other supernatural entities. She felt a kind of affinity to her classmates—she too was busy writing things and figuring things out. But she also felt that a rift existed between her and the rest of them, and that it was widening. She was becoming more and more detached from her surroundings. The real world kept slipping away, and once or twice, she had trouble bringing her attention back.

***

Name: The Forests of Tables, Benches, and Regret.

Danger Classification: Mostly harmless; may cause mild physical distress.

Description: The Forests of Tables, Benches, and Regret appear periodically underneath certain tables and benches, usually during the rainy season. The Forests are characterized by straight, polished trees and a thick mist that smothers the ground. When the table and bench legs appear more numerous than usual, this signals the coming of the Forests. One researcher went so far as to describe it as "feet for days", as the number of human legs and feet also seems to multiply.

Mode of Operation: Many of the GGHSS entities enjoy roaming the Forests as part of their self-care routine. However, the air is not particularly wholesome, and it is recommended not to spend more than 23 minutes there at a stretch. Those who have spent longer bouts of time have experienced deep feelings of regret for their own life and for everyone else's life as well. The Forests can be quite whimsical at times; they have been known to leave tiny clouds on the feet of seated students. However, the Forests are not altogether benign as they have been known to absorb certain girls. Research has been inconclusive as to what sort of girls are most at risk. The "trees" of the forests are also said to contain a jealous and malodorous sap, which causes painful blisters and feelings of great social anxiety when it comes into contact with bare skin.

***

Punishments at the GGHSS depended on how old the girl or girls were. Individual punishments for the very young were usually a sharp pinch. Older girls got a stinging slap across the face or a wooden ruler across the palm of the hand, with strict instructions not to flinch. Class punishments included kneeling with bare knees on the rough cement floor. Sometimes girls had to stand or kneel with their arms stretched straight above their heads; any wavering would result in the wooden ruler. When things were really bad, the entire class would be made to kneel with their arms above their heads, in the middle of the broken cement basketball court, right when the sun was at its height. Local trains would pass by, and young men would whistle or imitate their pose as the train went past. This form of punishment would only end when someone fainted.

That particular day had been like any other. The girls were not any louder or rowdier than usual, but the Chemistry Miss was in a very bad mood. The first time she came in to complain, she sharply admonished the class for being so loud. Prasanna was instructed to stand at the front and write down the names of the noisiest girls. The Chemistry Miss left. The noise continued. She returned, ordered everyone to kneel, and left again. The class continued to make noise and for some reason, nobody kneeled. It wasn't clear why; it seemed as if they had all decided that the Chemistry Miss didn't really mean it and would not be back again.

Unfortunately, she did come back again, and her terrible mood became even worse when she saw that no one was kneeling. She demanded to know why. A few voices said sorry, which made her even angrier. The entire class was then paraded down to the basketball court and made to kneel with their arms in the air. The Chemistry Miss went around to each girl, ensuring that her bare knees were touching the cracked cement floor. Then she left, leaving instructions that the girls were to remain kneeling for the entire period. Once she was gone, a dull silence descended. Someone would whisper something, someone else would say shush. It was a very hot day, and Thamarai could feel beads of sweat racing down her scalp and neck. The only thing to be done was to wait for someone to faint.

"*Maakaanu nenaikaathakka,*" sang Thamarai softly. "*Kekaama baathil sol akka.*"

"Hey," hissed S.T. Priya. "Shut your mouth, you'll get us caught."

"*Anjaatha ambalaya oru ponnu thedi vanthom, azhaga aadi paadi vanthom.*"

A number of girls shuffled and told Thamarai to shut up. Thamarai continued to sing.

"*Ava peru Neelaveni, nalla maama veetu rani.*"

"Hey loose-u. Crack. Shut your mouth," said S.T. Priya. "You think you are a great singer like P. Susheela, is it?"

"You sing now," said Thamarai.

"Oh really? You think I'm a crack like you, is it?"

"*Neelaveni,*" sang Thamarai.

"*Amma Ne-e-e-laveni,*" sang S.T. Priya, unable to resist the urge to break into song. "Good one, no?"

She began to chat with a few girls in a harsh whisper and Thamarai listened to the rest of the song play in her head. At the far edges of the school ground, mirages of water began to shimmer, then disappear every time Thamarai turned her head to look at them. Out of the corner of her eye, she could make out the rusted shape of Smiling Face, teetering on the edge of the largest mirage, surrounded by adoring girls. Thamarai watched it flip its head back, so its mouth was open to the sky. Clouds, birds, and insects disappeared inside it. Then, with a sudden splash, Smiling Face fell into the mirage.

At that same moment, two of Thamarai's classmates fainted with painful-sounding thumps onto the concrete floor. A few of the quicker girls immediately scooped the fallen students up and carried them to the classroom, while another girl got water from the pump and splashed it onto their faces. In a few seconds, the Chemistry Miss was back, frowning down on the rest of them.

"Fine, get back to class," she muttered begrudgingly. "But just let me hear one word from you."

The classroom was dark and cool after the heat of the basketball court. Thamarai could feel the familiar pain and back-and-forth pulsing in her head that sunstroke always brought on. She sat down and began to drink small sips of water. There were rumours that this kind of punishment was not supposed to be given to 12th standard girls. It was not proper to have young women kneeling in public like that with their arms up for everyone to see. This might be the last time she ever got punished this way.

But the thought did not really move Thamarai at all. With the rest of the class trying to keep their noise to a minimum, Thamarai put her head down and fell into a deep, peaceful slumber. It was the sweetest sleep she had had in a long time.

***

The Supernatural and You

Note: Slated for deletion. This section is marked for immediate removal as someone, possibly one of the volunteers, keeps putting it back in. Under no circumstances should this entry appear in this compendium. **It is completely unnecessary.**

Note 2: On behalf of the volunteers of AMUUF, I strongly condemn the insinuation that this section is being reinserted by volunteers. Please provide proof of the same

or desist from making these kinds of false accusations.
Note 3: Sorry dear, obviously AMUUF researchers and archivists have more important things to do.
Note 4: Sorry dear, so do the volunteers.
Note 5: Volunteers are an integral part of AMUUF and should be treated with respect.
Note 6: Volunteers are an integral part of your father-in-law's head.
Note 7: Friends, this is not a fish market.
Note 8: Oh my god.
Note 9: Please do not add any more notes to this section, the topic is closed!
Note 10: Let's leave a note demanding nobody leave any notes.
Note 11: FISH MARKET!
NOTE 12: STOP LEAVING NOTES WE ARE NOT KIDDING!
Note 13: AAAAARRRRRGGGGHHHHH!
Note 14: FISH MARKET!

Notes are no longer permitted for this section

Admin Note - Why is this section still in here?

A foray into the world of the supernatural GGHSS can be intensely personal. For those who are concerned about what the supernatural might mean to them, we ask that they consider who they are in the context of their own lives. Are you important to yourself? Do you engage in dangerous self-care activities? Are you vegetarian? Do you know where the Snowdens of yesteryear are? Engaging with the supernatural has often been likened to coming to terms with one's own homosexuality, in that these two things have nothing in common with each other. Do not ask what you can expect from the supernatural. Ask instead, what can the supernatural expect from you. Will you be pretty? Will you be rich? These are the kind of things that the supernatural likes, and the prettier and richer you are, the better it is for everyone. Researchers have noted with some surprise that one of the biggest questions people have regarding the supernatural in the GGHSS is whether it will make them gay. The answer is yes, it will absolutely make you very gay. If you are reading this right now, it is because you are gay.

***

11th standard proved to be the year that Prasanna and Thamarai parted ways. This was not totally unexpected. Everyone knew that Thamarai was Prasanna's fan, not her friend. And while the two girls did spend a lot of time together, it was perhaps not the strongest of bonds. Instead, it came across as one of those school romances; intensely felt by one person and completely forgotten by both once school was over.

Many were surprised to see that Thamarai and S.T. Priya did *not* part ways. After years of unhappy interactions between the two girls, it seemed only natural that they would eventually split. Some relationships were not healthy to carry from childhood into adulthood, and Thamarai and S.T. Priya had always felt like they had been forced to be friends. S.T. Priya's repeated barbs at Thamarai and Thamarai's uncanny way of pressing S.T. Priya's buttons seemed to mask a clinginess between them. Both were lost, holding on to each other as they tried to navigate the world.

As the impending study holidays crept closer, S.T. Priya felt a keen sense of elation from answering the dummy question papers. While she hadn't mastered all the subjects, she was doing quite well in a number of them, and for the first time, her papers were being borrowed and studied by the others. While S.T. Priya had never felt jealous of Prasanna, she had always felt miles behind her. Now, it appeared that the two were on nearly equal ground. The thought of being one of the more academically successful girls without mutating into an anxiety-and-diarrhoea-riddled first-bencher filled S.T. Priya with a heady feeling. She felt like she was bursting with wisdom that simply had to be shared. Unfortunately, the only person available was Thamarai.

S.T. Priya had always wondered about Thamarai. She knew Thamarai was genuinely lost, not just in academics but in everything. She seemed even more lost now, and sometimes, even when sitting right next to her, S.T. Priya would forget she was there. It felt like Thamarai was dissolving into something that S.T. Priya could not see. She always had her head buried in the old botany record notebook—except when Prasanna was around.

"Tell me what's in that record notebook," S.T. Priya asked one day. "I promise to listen this time."

"No," said Thamarai.

"Let me see it then."

Thamarai paused, then handed it over, knowing that, as with Prasanna, S.T. Priya would only be able to see the botany notes and diagrams.

S.T. Priya looked through a few pages, frowned, and handed it back.

"*You're* seeing something in this though," said S.T. Priya accusingly. "Just tell me what you're seeing."

"No."

"So, you are seeing something."

"No."

"Don't lie."

"Okay I'm seeing something. Pothuma?"

"You're seeing your grandfather's head."

"Seri."

"Why do I do it? Why do I keep talking to you and doing this to myself?"

"I don't know."

"Even I don't know."

S.T. Priya went back to fidgeting with her pen. It was precisely this aspect of Thamarai that irritated her so much. She never gave a straight answer for anything and always managed to turn the conversation around in a way that caused maximum irritation. No matter how she tried, S.T. Priya was not able to let this go. She had known Thamarai for a few years, and yet she did not know her at all. She decided to keep a closer eye on her; she wasn't sure what she would discover, but she hoped she would get some insight.

For a few weeks, nothing untoward happened. Thamarai came to school, ate lunch, read her notebook, and went home without much deviation. Then one day, word came that the PT Misses would be busy all day, as they were going to teach physical training drills on the assembly grounds. Thamarai decided to take this opportunity to try and reach the Phantom First Floor again. When there was no teacher present and everyone seemed duly occupied, Thamarai slipped out of the classroom and made her way to the staircase. What she didn't know was that S.T. Priya was following close behind her, not even trying to be covert about her spying operation.

"Hey, what's this, where are you all going?" said Prasanna. She was sitting in the corridor, watching Thamarai and S.T. Priya pass.

"The loose is off somewhere," said S.T. Priya in a very loud whisper. "I'm going to see where."

Prasanna watched them go, then called out, "Shall I also come?"

"Come, come!" S.T. Priya called back.

Prasanna quickly closed her book and got up. The truth was that she was feeling a bit bored, and following Thamarai to wherever she was going seemed strangely exciting.

They both followed Thamarai then paused, watching her ascend the stairs at a light run. S.T. Priya followed her, then Prasanna, but before the latter could reach the top, Thamarai was on her way down again, brow furrowed, staring intently at the ground. Prasanna stood to the side, watching with interest as Thamarai ran up and down, followed by S.T. Priya, who was getting increasingly annoyed.

"Hey, stop it now, you crack," said S.T. Priya, finally fed up. Thamarai noticed her with a start.

"Why are you both here?" she asked.

"We're following you," said S.T. Priya. "Wanted to see what crack things you do during the day. Like going up and down the stairs like a loose."

"I'm not simply going up and down the stairs."

"Where are you going?" asked Prasanna.

Thamarai chewed her bottom lip thoughtfully. "I am going upstairs," she said finally.

"You're already upstairs," said Prasanna gently.

"Oh. Are there any more steps?"

"Yes," said S.T. Priya. "They are on my head as you can see."

"Then I am going downstairs," said Thamarai, and down she went with S.T. Priya and Prasanna in close pursuit. Once they were down, she gave them both an awkward look and made her way up the stairs again.

"Hey idiot! Are you crazy?" said S.T. Priya. "No seriously I'm asking, have you gone insane?"

"No."

"Why are you going up and down like this?" asked Prasanna.

"What?"

"Yenna what? My chappal will break if I hit you," said S.T. Priya.

Thamarai slipped past them and rushed up the stairs again. S.T. Priya ran after her, followed by Prasanna, who decided to walk this time. Thamarai took two steps at a time, wondering what she was going to tell them when she reached the top. Perhaps she could say she had forgotten something? She could say that she kept forgetting one thing after the other, which was why she had to keep going up and down.

She reached the top of the stairs and lurched to a stop. She looked around and felt that same hollow, abandoned feeling she had felt before. She had finally reached the Phantom First Floor. She looked behind her and saw that she had also brought S.T. Priya and Prasanna with her.

***

The last time Thamarai had been on the Phantom First Floor, only Prasanna had been with her, and Prasanna had not seen anything mysterious or unworldly. It had not struck her as strange that the entire floor seemed to be devoid of people. She had simply walked along the right wing, found the wayward attendance register, and made her way back downstairs again.

But this time it was different. Thamarai could tell that both of them looked uncomfortable and confused, that something had struck them as not quite right.

"Seri, you've come upstairs, no? Now come back down," said Prasanna, turning to descend.

"No thank you," said Thamarai, pulling away. "I have some work here."

"What work here? You don't have any work here, come on."

Thamarai turned resolutely and made her way to the right-hand wing. She wasn't sure when the floor would send her back down of its own accord, and did not want to waste any time.

In one classroom, she saw a swarm of butterflies fluttering in the corner of the ceiling. A dark liquid was dripping out from under them, and she quickly moved on, unwilling to see what the liquid actually was.

"Hey! Wait for me," said a harsh whisper. S.T. Priya grabbed Thamarai's arm and held it like a vice. She followed Thamarai closely as they walked on. Prasanna came behind them, eyes wide, looking around in utter bewilderment.

"What is this?" whispered S.T. Priya.

"First floor," said Thamarai, not wanting to scare her more than necessary. "Why?"

"This is not the first floor," said S.T. Priya, looking around. "Where is everybody?"

"Who?"

"What is that?" asked Prasanna. She was pointing to a balloon-like infestation of Little Nightmares that had almost devoured an entire classroom. Thamarai quickly grabbed her arm and pulled both girls along with her.

They continued quietly down the corridor which, like last time, seemed endless. After they had passed a number of empty classrooms in succession, S.T. Priya began to calm down a little. But she would still not let go of Thamarai's arm.

"You've been here before," said S.T. Priya accusingly.

"Just once," Thamarai lied.

She did not want to engage in conversation at the moment. She had seen a smiling young man, a Cine Hero, walking out of a classroom towards them. He was looking at them with such love and hope in his eyes that Thamarai had gasped. Prasanna had stopped completely and Thamarai had to pull her along.

"Who was that?" asked S.T. Priya, looking back.

"No one. Come on."

They continued down the hall at a quicker pace. The more they walked, the more Thamarai wished she had stayed in class. Coming here alone was one thing, but coming with these two was just a bad idea.

"Hey!" said S.T. Priya suddenly. "Get back to your class. What are you doing up here?"

Thamarai yelped. This was something seniors often said to their juniors, simply because they could. If they saw a junior walking in the corridors at an odd time, many seniors decided they were well within their rights to demand that the young people head back to class or head home, whichever was applicable. S.T. Priya had spotted a small girl wearing a pink and white dress, breathing through her mouth and watching them intently.

The hole where her eye should have been looked puckered and sunken; it was leaking a pus-like yellow liquid.

S.T. Priya seemed not to notice. "Hey, I'm talking to you," she said peevishly.

"Is it your birthday?" asked Prasanna more kindly. Ammani refused to answer Prasanna, or to comply with S.T. Priya's wishes. S.T. Priya's fear had been replaced with indignation at being insulted.

Thamarai could guess why Ammani was there: she wanted her eye back.

"Akka..." said Ammani.

"Yenna akka? What are you doing here?" demanded S.T. Priya.

Thamarai began to run, pulling Prasanna along with her. "Come on! Don't stand there!" she shouted back.

S.T. Priya stood for a second, confused. Then she started running too. The faster they ran, the faster Ammani seemed to catch up with them, and the sound of her saying "Akka" was scaring Thamarai more than she cared to admit. She had Ammani's eye in her kerchief. It occurred to her that all she probably needed to do was drop it, and Ammani would stop following them.

The girls ran past the stairwell and down the left wing. Just as they were about to pass a classroom, Thamarai took a sharp turn inside, pulling Prasanna along with her. S.T. Priya followed and they all stood with their backs against the wall, panting heavily. They could hear Ammani getting closer, breathing through her mouth. They held their breath as Ammani paused in front of the classroom. For a moment it looked like she was going to come inside, but she didn't; instead she made her way down the endless corridor, breathing out the word "akka" every so often.

Thamarai peeked out, saw that Ammani was now a tiny speck in the far distance, and breathed a sigh of relief.

"We better be careful going back," Thamarai said. "She will be looking for us."

"Isn't she..." said Prasanna, looking confused. "She looks like—I mean haven't I seen her..."

"Yes," said Thamarai. She turned around to view the rest of the classroom. It was the one where she had met Gopalan Sir earlier. And there he was, sitting in the same place, watching the girls with a look of hope.

***

For some reason, seeing Gopalan Sir on the Phantom First Floor made sense to Prasanna and S.T. Priya. Neither of them questioned it or asked what he was doing there. Prasanna smiled broadly at him and inquired about his family and health.

"Not so good ma," said Gopalan Sir. "I feel very tired. But I'm not able to rest."

He did seem more distressed than he had before. Thamarai thought he looked like he was carrying something heavy in his heart. She took a seat in front of him, and S.T. Priya and Prasanna sat beside her.

"What is troubling you sir? You can tell us," Thamarai asked. He sighed and rubbed his face. He looked so tired that she was not sure if he would be able to say anything.

"You know one thing?" he finally said. "I used to work here in this school. Many years ago. It was my first job ma, and I was very keen to do well. When I was working here, I would see this old woman standing outside the school gates every evening. I thought she was waiting to pick up her grandchild, though I never saw any girl go with her. I felt she shouldn't stand there alone like that. She was elderly and it wasn't right, making her stand in the road. But she wouldn't come into the school grounds. She would just smile and say *parava illai sir, naan inge nikkuren*. But I couldn't let it go. I insisted. One day, she finally relented and followed me in. I asked her to stand in the shade, and said *Isn't this better? Aren't you glad you came in? You're glad you listened to me, isn't it?* Arrogant fellow that I was. She just nodded, but I could see something dark had crossed her face.

Next day I saw her again, this time standing inside the school grounds, but she already looked sick. The wrinkles on her face seemed to be multiplying, and her skin had started to look grey. I kept telling her that it was better she wait inside, and she would just nod at me. Many days went by and she seemed to be getting thinner. She no longer smiled like she used to when she saw me. I kept telling her to send someone else to pick up her granddaughter, why was she doing this to herself in her old age? She never said anything, just stood there.

"Then one Sunday I came to school to pick up some papers for correction. And I saw her still standing, in the same spot. Wrinkles had now covered her entire face and I could barely see her eyes and nose. Only her mouth remained visible—but it did not look like a mouth, more like a gash had been torn into her face. I felt uncomfortable, seeing her like that. But when I tried to talk to her, she would not reply. She was looking very unwell by now. I tried to buy her something to eat, but she wouldn't take anything. So, I stood there with her. Someone would surely come, isn't it? I thought someone at her home would notice she was gone and come looking for her. And they would tell me, *Oh she does this all the time! She will wander off and one of us must come and take her home.* How I wished something like that would happen. But no one came. It became darker. You know ma, I have been in many forest places and caves when I was a youngster. None of them filled me with such dread as the school that night. I kept seeing strange things and it seemed like the paati was changing right in front of my eyes. At some point, I just left. I had a wife and child at home. I was scared. I was scared and I wanted to go home.

"Well, I would keep seeing her, usually at the end of the day, standing in the same place. I would try to talk to her, coax her to eat; nothing. One day I tried to take her hand and that's when I saw it: she had seven fingers, not five. And I don't know why, but the minute I saw that, I felt so cold and alone. I felt like the world was on the outside, living its life, but I was stuck here with this woman and I couldn't do anything. Eventually I couldn't stand it anymore. I went to school again on a Sunday and there she was, standing as always. She looked like she was about to fall down. This time I didn't waste a second; I picked her up, placed her on my cycle in front of me, and set off for home. She weighed nothing and I remember cycling so fast. This was just after I had lost my own grandmother. I was having soft feelings, I knew that. And I wasn't thinking clearly. But when I got home, my wife prepared our extra room, put a mat and pillow, an extra sari, and I kept the paati in that room. I laid her down on the mat. She wouldn't eat, didn't drink anything. Sometimes she would get up and try to crawl into the corners of the room. Sometimes she even tried to climb up the walls. But at night, that was when it was worst. When we closed the door to that room so she could sleep, we heard such terrible noises. It was like someone was being beaten, then strangled. Sometimes she would sing in a voice that made my blood run cold. The insects, lizards all ran out of that room. Nothing would go inside. But whenever I went in to check, the paati would just be lying there as always. I sent my wife and child to her mother's house and for one crazy week, I stayed in that house alone. I took leave from work. During the days, I would sit and watch her sleeping or whatever it was she was doing. Then in the nights, I would close the door and listen to all the terrible sounds that came from inside. It was the worst time of my life, ma.

"I would like to say I figured something out and fixed everything, or that I was able to conquer whatever evil I had brought into the house, but I didn't. One morning when I opened the door, she wasn't there. I mean, I could no longer see her, but I knew she was still in the room. I could feel it. The walls, the floor, everything seemed to be haunted by something terrible. She was still in there. Even now, I wonder if she still… but no, that can't be. Anyway, I waited one week. She never came back. I didn't need any coaxing; I quit my job, immediately found another place, and moved my family out of that house. I kept telling myself that she must have gone to her own home, that I couldn't be responsible if she left of her own accord.

"I never saw her again. Sometimes I wondered, was it my fault? Should I have just left her alone, at the side of the road? Was it wrong to bring her inside the school? Was it wrong to bring her home? I was only trying to help but… it has been gnawing at me all my life. Initially, my wife was worried about her too, but I told her that the paati's people had come to take her, so she would not have to worry."

"I have carried this alone. Now I just wish I could tell her I'm sorry. I hope it wasn't something I did that made everything go wrong."

The story left very different impressions on the girls. Prasanna was visibly upset. It touched her deeply, and she felt for both Gopalan Sir and the paati. S.T. Priya realized that Thamarai had been right; the mysterious room had indeed been haunted. Thamarai was overcome with waves of guilt. She realized with some dismay that she had killed Gopalan Sir's paati. Not own-paati, but still, it was bad.

"Oh, *that* paati," said Thamarai. She had no idea why she said this. Gopalan Sir blinked at her.

"You know who I mean?" he asked.

"Sure," said Thamarai, trying to sound nonchalant and hearty. "I remember that paati very well. I used to see her all the time."

"But this happened years ago," said Gopalan Sir.

"Of course. Of course, yes you are right. What I meant to say was I have heard about her. Her family lived near S.T. Priya's old house. Which is your old house also. Isn't that interesting?"

"Are you sure it was her?"

"Of course! I know exactly who you are talking about."

"Do you know what happened to her?" asked Gopalan Sir a little weakly.

"Nothing! She was fine! She was staying with some relations nearby. You're right, sometimes she wandered. You don't worry about anything."

Thamarai thought Gopalan Sir was looking a bit more transparent than before. He seemed to be deep in thought. "I always wanted to apologize to her. I should never have forced her to come into the grounds," he said.

"It's okay sir, you don't have to worry about all that."

Gopalan Sir frowned a little. He didn't seem totally convinced.

"I have heard of that paati too," Prasanna blurted out. "We all know about her. You don't worry."

Thamarai wasn't sure why Prasanna was corroborating her lie, but it seemed to be doing the trick. Gopalan Sir sighed. His shoulders relaxed and he took off his glasses, wiped his face with his handkerchief. He was much more transparent now; she could almost see through him.

"Well, that is good then," he said and stood up. The girls

watched as he left the room and walked into the open corridor. He stood there for a while, watching the afternoon sun paint the bushes and the side of the building. Thamarai could see dragonflies hovering inside his head. In a few seconds, he had disappeared completely.

They left the room and began walking down the corridor where Ammani had vanished. Prasanna took Thamarai's hand and walked beside her.

"You both don't have to come with me you know," said Thamarai. "You can go back."

"We know," said S.T. Priya. The girls carried on down the corridor together.

***

It was a truly impressive thing. S.T. Priya could be in the most magical place, a place fraught with supernatural energy, possibility, and wonder, and still be the same girl who was always passing sarcastic comments. She was now making random gibes about Thamarai and the scenery. The more they walked, the more S.T. Priya complained, saying that nothing interesting was happening, and surely it was a waste of time to just walk around here endlessly. Prasanna held Thamarai's hand tightly and quietly looked around her as if she was walking through a haunted house. Even the most mundane objects appeared to be harbouring terrible secrets.

"This place is useless," said S.T. Priya. "Let's go back, I'm hungry."

"It's not useless," said Thamarai.

"Oh, don't start," said S.T. Priya dismissively. "As if this is some big Maya Bazaar. Nothing very special has happened so far."

"What about Gopalan Sir?" asked Thamarai, a little exasperated. "You heard his story. You saw him!"

"So?"

Thamarai shook her head and sighed. Of all the people in the world to share in her secret of the supernatural goings-on at the GGHSS, S.T. Priya was the last person she would have chosen. She was dismissive enough about real-world things. To think that she was now privy to all this magic made Thamarai feel a little angry.

"Why don't you go back?" said Thamarai. "There's nothing for you here."

"Why don't you be quiet?" said S.T. Priya, peeping into an empty classroom. She was looking for some kind of souvenir to take back with her. So far, she had found nothing, not a piece of chalk, not a bobby pin. She had tried to break off the shell of a Little Nightmare; Thamarai had almost let her do it, but had stopped her at the last minute.

Thamarai watched as S.T. Priya wandered into another empty classroom.

Then she turned and began heading back to class. She had had enough. S.T. Priya could make her own way downstairs. Prasanna let go of her hand and fell back.

"Come on," said Thamarai, turning towards her.

"We can't just leave her here," said Prasanna.

"Why not?"

"Thamarai!" said Prasanna. "We can't."

"She can come down on her own, it's not such a big thing. Just come on, I'm…" She trailed off. Prasanna's face had frozen into a look of shock. Thamarai turned around and stared. Standing there, looking at the two girls, was the English Sir.

***

The silence was broken by S.T. Priya, running up to them, holding a sizeable broken piece of concrete. She, too, froze the minute she saw the English Sir. He looked quietly menacing, standing perfectly still, the shadow of a smile hovering over his lips. He slowly folded his arms, and Thamarai realized that he had no idea where he was. He seemed to be oblivious to the energy that permeated the place.

"What are you all doing here?" he asked softly.

Thamarai began to feel uneasy. There was something about the way he was standing that made her feel uncomfortable. A smirk slowly spread over his face.

"Sir, sorry sir," said Prasanna.

"So, the respected Prasanna is finally caught," he said with a slight drawl. He stared at her steadily, letting his gaze drop down to her chest. He seemed to be savouring the moment. He looked over at S.T. Priya, who was standing there with her mouth open and the chunk of concrete in her hands.

"And you're S.T. Sir's daughter aren't you," he said. He looked her up and down, causing her to drop the concrete. "And you," he said, turning to Thamarai. He gave her a small smile. He remembered her.

"Thamarai, sir," she said, feeling the words stick in her throat.

"What are you doing here?"

Thamarai tried to think of the movie she had seen last Sunday night. She tried to think of her aunt, even the sisters who had mysteriously disappeared. It was no use. *He remembers what he did,* she thought to herself.

Anger began to grow inside her. As scary as the Phantom First Floor could be, this was her turf. What right did he have to just saunter in like he owned it?

"Are you deaf? I asked you a question," said the English Sir, spitting out the words with a slight snarl.

"What are *you* doing here?" demanded Thamarai. "Porikki." Something like courage was filling her heart, spilling over into her muscles. She felt she had the upper hand here. Maybe she could do whatever she wanted to him. The thought made her giddy.

The English Sir smiled; he almost looked excited. "How's that, how's that? Say again?" he asked with a soft chuckle.

Thamarai took a step forward. "Don't try all that here," she said. "This isn't your place."

The English Sir begin to laugh. It wasn't a forced laugh. He actually thought what Thamarai had said was funny.

"You're not speaking very respectfully." He almost whispered this, his voice tense and taut.

"Why should I be respectful to you?" said Thamarai. "Were you respectful to me when you touched me? Was that what a respectable man does?" She turned to the other two girls. They both looked completely appalled.

"Oh! I'm very scared of this one," laughed the English Sir, putting his hands up. Then just as suddenly he was glaring at her, his voice so soft, almost gentle. "Don't worry," he said. "I can teach you to be respectful."

Thamarai laughed. Something tremendous was flowing through her, a headiness that was almost leaving her breathless.

She was going to punish the English Sir. It would completely change him. She thought of the movie climaxes where the hero would pace back and forth, delivering fiery dialogue that made everyone in the theatre clap and whistle.

"Dei don't we all know about you, porikki. Such a great man. Treats all the girls with such respect. You fucker," Thamarai said.

The English Sir stared at her.

"What did you say?"

"Fucker," shouted Thamarai. "Fucker fucker fucker!"

"Thamarai," hissed Prasanna.

"Fucker!"

It seemed that now that she had started, she couldn't stop saying it.

"Keep that up," he said softly, lingering on each word as if it was something delicious. "And see what happens to you."

"Oh, look at this!" said Thamarai. "Big man is going to do something. Are you going to touch me again? Put a finger on me and I'll take care of you, just see. This isn't your place."

Let him try touching her now. She would break every finger in his hand, snapping each one slowly, making him watch. She was so caught up in her thoughts that when she fell back, she had no idea what had happened. Somehow, she had tumbled against the wall and was now on the floor. Pain was running all through her head and neck. Her face felt very cold, then very hot. She could feel her cheek swelling.

The English Sir had slapped her.

S.T. Priya and Prasanna were both standing there, staring. Thamarai did not expect them to do anything. This was often the way when a girl got punished in front of others. She would bear her punishment. Others would watch. Everything would be still. There was something about silently witnessing violence that somehow made it worse.

"Get up," said the English Sir. He was clenching his teeth, opening and closing his fists. Thamarai got up. She was dizzy and her shoulders were hurting. She thought that was odd, to have aching shoulders after someone had slapped you across the face. The second slap came quickly on the other cheek. Everything hurt now. She had not expected the English Sir to be so strong. She stayed on the ground this time. He just stood there, looking at her, a dribble of spit hanging from his moustache.

"Put your kerchief to your nose," he ordered. Thamarai did as she was told. She held the cloth to her face, feeling the lump of Ammani's eye knotted in the corner. She was surprised by how much blood there was.

"Don't you eat?" asked the English Sir, rubbing one of his hands. "If you eat rice properly you won't bleed so much."

Her handkerchief was almost soaked through. Prasanna nipped towards her and gave her her own.

"Fucker, is it? I should kick you," the English Sir said thoughtfully. He was smiling, and his entire body was tensed, like he was about to explode.

"Sir she doesn't know what she's saying," said Prasanna in a shaky voice. "Please let her go."

Thamarai felt her stomach drop inside her. Her shoulders slumped and seemed to sink further into the floor. Everything had gone wrong. The upper hand was still his, as always. It would always be his. It had been silly for Thamarai to think that things would be different, just because they were happening on the Phantom First Floor.

That was when she noticed that the English Sir was standing right in front of the doorway of a classroom. She was sure there had been a solid wall there a few seconds ago. She froze. Inside, she could see the class of 9D. The room extended endlessly into darkness, with rows and rows of small, silent girls, sitting cross-legged with straight backs, their eyes fixed ahead of them. Black shadows gathered in the corners and near the ceiling, and it seemed hollow and cold; even the usual infestations of Little Nightmares were missing.

"What do you think?" said the English Sir, almost brightly. "Should I kick you?"

"So stupid," said Thamarai. "Who will say they want to be kicked?"

What happened next seemed to occur in slow motion. Thamarai saw the English Sir's face and realized he was going to hit her again. She stumbled upright. With whatever energy she could muster, she charged the English Sir. Her plan had been to push him into 9D. She wasn't sure what would happen to him there. There was a good chance that the legions of silent girls would do nothing. The English Sir might just walk out of the classroom unscathed and go on hitting her. But something might happen. Maybe 9D would peel the skin from his body. Maybe they would liquefy him into a small, black puddle.

Thamarai rammed into him, hurling the full force of her body into his stomach. But all he did was take a few steps back.

She was sure he would come after her now. She stumbled against the wall, and waited for him to hit her. But something in the classroom had caught his attention. He briskly walked into the room; nothing happened to him. He was frowning, slowly surveying the class with surprised but angry eyes. He looked down at the small, silent, identical girls and the teacher's table.

"What class is this?" he demanded. None of the girls made a sound.

"It's 9D sir," said Thamarai, rubbing her neck. The English Sir continued to frown as he scanned the room. The number of girls was endless; no one was moving or breathing. The usual smirk and self-assurance was draining from the English Sir's face. He looked confused, almost overwhelmed. He seemed to have forgotten about the three girls in the corridor.

"Let's go," Thamarai whispered to the other girls.

She began to make her way slowly towards the stairwell. Prasanna followed her, then S.T. Priya, the two of them looking dazed. They had almost crossed the 9D classroom when Thamarai noticed something blocking their way, right at the end of the corridor.

It was Ammani.

***

The entity looked larger than usual, a raspy, choking sound oozing from her open mouth; there was nowhere to go. S.T. Priya silently began to cry, while Prasanna grabbed Thamarai's arm. Thamarai took a breath and closed her eyes. She tried to steel herself against whatever was going to happen, but she felt limp. Her shoulders and face were throbbing with pain. Whatever happened, she was just going to take it. She had no energy to do anything else. It was definitely not a good idea to retreat into 9D. Ammani was a known evil; but there was no telling what she would do to get her eye back.

Thamarai's hand went to her handkerchief. It was still damp. She unwrapped the eye and rolled it between her thumb and forefinger, feeling the slight give. She held it up.

"What are you doing?" hissed Prasanna. An unsettling chittering noise began to come from the end of the corridor. Ammani had seen the eye. She began to run towards them, her teeth slightly bared, her remaining eye wide and unblinking while the empty socket gaped open. For some reason, she seemed to be running very slowly.

Thamarai waited until Ammani was close enough. Then she quickly threw the eye into 9D. Ammani spun around and ran into the classroom, where the English Sir was staring at her. Thamarai wasted no time. She slammed the door, latched it, and pressed herself against it to keep it shut.

She could hear the sound of the English Sir inside, demanding to be let out. But there were other noises as well; a rustling, the wheezing sound of Ammani breathing through her mouth, the sound of a class of young girls quietly repeating something in unison. The door shook, as the English Sir punched it violently from the other side. She wondered what was happening to him, what he was seeing.

"Come on!" she said to the other two as the shaking became more intense. "Help me!"

S.T. Priya began to cry louder. Prasanna stood there without moving.

"Help me!" shouted Thamarai.

"Open the door!" said Prasanna. Thamarai stared at her. "Open the door Thamarai," she repeated.

"What? Why?" demanded Thamarai.

She felt a knot of anger rise in her throat. She didn't care if Prasanna had said it; it was a stupid idea, and she was not going to do it. She would not open the door.

Prasanna watched her for a few seconds, then lurched forward and began prying Thamarai away from the door.

For a second, Thamarai could not believe what was happening. By the time she started fighting back, it was already too late. She had been pulled off and shoved into the opposite wall.

"Why?" she shouted, almost in tears. "Do you know what he did to me? Doesn't that mean anything? You're a girl, aren't you?"

Prasanna did not seem to hear her. She quickly opened the latch. The English Sir tumbled out and fell on the floor. His eyes were closed, but he did not look bloodied or hurt; his breathing was a little short and his left hand was trembling, but apart from that, there seemed to be nothing wrong with him. The classroom was empty and quiet: Ammani and 9D had both disappeared.

The three girls looked at the English Sir.

S.T. Priya finally stopped crying. Thamarai felt a fist of rage flex inside her throat. She couldn't move. Hot, angry tears were flowing down her face. Her mouth felt dry and salty and her head was throbbing so painfully she felt like screaming. She had never felt this much rage in her life. There had been one chance, and she was the only one who had tried to do something. No one had been on her side. Even Prasanna hadn't tried to help her. She had helped the English Sir instead.

Thamarai spun around and made her way to the stairwell, without waiting for the other girls.

***

When she got back to class, she saw that she had only been gone for an hour. It had been a free period and most of the girls had been absorbed with the dummy question papers. No one even noticed she had been gone. Thamarai's face, which had been bloodied by the English Sir on the Phantom First Floor, looked fine now, but it still hurt. Her head, neck, and shoulders were all pulsing with pain.

S.T. Priya and Prasanna walked into the classroom a few minutes after her. Prasanna went straight to her bag, pulled out her physics text and rough notebook, and headed to the corridor. S.T. Priya began chatting with the girls who sat behind her, as if nothing had happened. Every so often she would glance at the window or corridor. *She's looking for him,* Thamarai thought to herself. This made her angry too, but in a dull, blunted kind of way. *She's worried he might be dead.* Even if he was, there was no way someone would connect his death to three 11A girl students. It was ludicrous to think that a few girls could do anything to a man like the English Sir.

Thamarai began watching the window as well. She was curious, more than anything. If he did return, would he remember what had happened to him? Would he be okay?

Then, a few minutes after the final bell rang, there he was. Striding down the corridor, his face in that same slight smirk. He seemed perfectly normal. He strode past the classroom, not even turning his head to look inside, calling out to some smaller girls to go home and not loiter in the hallways. Thamarai and S.T. Priya exchanged a quick look. S.T. Priya sighed with relief. When she had packed her bag and was about to leave, Thamarai turned to her and asked in a low voice, "Are you okay?

"Yeah," said S.T. Priya. "Are *you* okay?"

Thamarai felt tears brim in her eyes. She was so, so tired. And everything had gone wrong. The best opportunity had presented itself and nothing had happened. Everything was just as bad as it had always been.

A few days later, Thamarai rummaged through her bag and realized that the record notebook was gone. She slowly walked around the classroom, checking under tables and benches, but the notebook was not to be found. Its loss saddened her. It had come into her life on its own accord and now it had left in the same way. Maybe what had happened on the Phantom First Floor had caused it to disappear. Or maybe its time had simply come.

She sat still as the rest of the class buzzed around her. Now there was nothing to do. She looked over at Prasanna, who was reviewing maths sums with another girl. S.T. Priya was singing "Madrasa Suthi Paaka Poren" in a tune that seemed to be wholly of her own invention.

Lighthouse-il yeri nikka poren naan
Mangaatha rani pola varen

Thamarai listened to the song for a few seconds. Then she put her head down and went to sleep.

***

Life without the botany record notebook was difficult to get used to. Thamarai had a lot of free time on her hands now. She could think of nothing else to do, so she put a lot of effort into appearing like she was studying. She underlined things, wrote them over and over again in her notebook. Her old talent of making up diagrams and tables still held strong.

She found that she could not write about supernatural entities anymore. When she did put pen to paper, she ended up writing pages and pages of tiny dashes. To her dismay, she found that she was beginning to forget much of what she had read in the notebook as well. It was like her brain was a sieve and anything relating to the supernatural was quietly pouring out. It only occurred to her later that she probably wasn't seeing anything supernatural anymore either. Now that she thought about it, she could not remember the last time she had seen a Sand Worm or a Sex Demon. She was forgetting what many of these things looked like. The telltale shape of the Little Nightmares, Ammani, everything was getting mixed up, then fading away.

Relations between S.T. Priya and Thamarai remained mostly the same, except for one marked difference. S.T. Priya's barbed comments had completely stopped. In fact, the two girls hardly spoke at all when they were together. For a while, Thamarai waited, expecting Prasanna to come to her with an apology. One day she asked S.T. Priya about it, and S.T. Priya shook her head.

"She won't apologize to you."

"After what she did? Really?"

"She doesn't think she did anything wrong. In fact, she thinks you should apologize."

Thamarai stared. "*Me*?"

"Just leave it Thamarai. This won't be resolved. You both believe different things."

"Isn't he a porikki? Doesn't he deserve some kind of punishment?"

"I agree," said S.T. Priya. "But what can you do?"

Thamarai watched Prasanna that day, but Prasanna would not even look at her. It was like she was trying to cut out Thamarai's presence from the scope of her everyday life. Thamarai did not feel as heartbroken about this as she would have expected. She felt alone and isolated, and still a little angry at Prasanna. But that was all slowly fading, leaving behind a feeling of disappointment. She was disappointed in Prasanna, more than anything.

Soon the school closed for study holidays. These proved to be worse than school; the house was dusty, hot, and oppressive, and was currently home to a number of wasps. Even when Thamarai was sitting and doing nothing, wasps stung her on her feet and arms. One morning, S.T. Priya called her and suggested they study together. Thamarai refused at first. Then three wasps stung her in quick succession and she changed her mind. She gathered her books.

After getting lost a few times, she finally found the address, tucked away in a lane so narrow it could only accommodate pedestrians and cyclists. S.T. Priya met her at the door. Her new house was smaller than the old one, but brighter and cosier; it was a portion of a larger, older home, which meant that the inside was always cool.

"I knew you would get lost," said S.T. Priya. "Everyone gets lost the first time they come. After a few times it becomes easy to remember."

They both settled in the main room, under a small, rickety ceiling fan. S.T. Priya put out multiple pens, pencils, a ruler, dummy question papers, and her textbooks.

"Oh, you're actually studying ah?" said Thamarai

"Then?" said S.T. Priya with surprise.

"I came just for time pass. My house is so hot and wasps keep stinging me."

"Okay," said S.T. Priya. "But don't make too much noise, there are people sleeping in the other portions of the house."

Thamarai nodded and looked at some old copies of *Kalki* and *Kumudam*. Then she watched S.T. Priya as she wrote out elaborate answers, underlined things, crossed things out and rewrote them.

"Have you finished covering everything?" Thamarai asked.

"No way," said S.T. Priya with a laugh. "I study something then I forget it next day. That's why I have to keep at it."

"I'm worried about how badly I'm going to fail," said Thamarai.

S.T. Priya stared at her. "Really?" she said. "I thought you didn't care."

"I don't. But sometimes I feel bad about my studies. And I think, what future can there be for me?"

"You're not meant for studying, Thamarai. Just leave it," said S.T. Priya. She didn't say it in a consoling kind of way. It was more like she was stating a fact.

"Do you think I'm meant for something else?" asked Thamarai.

S.T. Priya shook her head. "I don't know what is going to happen to you."

***

Thamarai went to S.T. Priya's house every day for the rest of the study holidays. While S.T. Priya studied, Thamarai would first walk about the small garden that was in the front yard. Then she would come back inside and drink a big glass of water slowly. After that, she would lie on her back and stare at the ceiling. It was criss-crossed with old wooden beams. On the lower beams, she could see a few old tins that had probably been kept there for storage, then been forgotten. Toffees, fountain pens, old letters, coins; anything could be in those tins. Thamarai wondered why they had been forgotten. She would think about the tins and eventually fall into a deep slumber.

Then came lunch, after which S.T. Priya would take a small break with her. S.T. Priya would pull out some of her older songbooks and sing the hits of MGR and Sivaji Ganesan while Thamarai listened. At around four p.m., S.T. Priya would make them both some coffee. Then Thamarai would head home.

Once, Thamarai asked about Prasanna.

"Has she ever asked about me?"

S.T. Priya shook her head.

"She doesn't like talking about what happened," she said. "Or about you."

Thamarai nodded. This hurt to hear, but not very badly. It occurred to her that she would probably never talk to Prasanna again, not even during 12th. She could not remember the last thing she had said to her. And even though Thamarai had been slapped and attacked, so much of that day was starting to slip from her memory. S.T. Priya didn't like to talk about it either but when pressed, she admitted that she too was forgetting most of it. She hoped that one day, she would forget it completely.

11th standard exams eventually came around. The girls all pretended not to take them seriously, to have come simply to mark attendance. But they all stayed to the end of each one, writing numerous pages of answers and discussing them afterwards. Unlike the others, Thamarai sat for the minimum required time, handed in a blank answer sheet, and went home. It seemed like such a waste, cycling in the searing heat to sit for a paper that she would not write and that the teachers would not mark.

One day, she reached home from the chemistry exam to find the sisters once again. For some reason, her first thought was that they had been kidnapped and had now been returned, only to find out that their house was missing. The whole family had come in an auto and were looking over the empty plot. The mother and father looked smaller in the sun but the sisters looked well-fed and vibrant.

"We told you about this how many times," they said, eyeing her narrowly.

"Yes, yes so many times," said Thamarai.

"And yet you still seem surprised to see us."

"Chee, nothing like that."

"So, you know that we tore down the old house and have been staying in town until the new house is built. Right?"

"Of course, I knew all that."

"Really? You don't look like you know anything. It's like we are telling you all this for the first time."

"Haha."

"Yenna haha."

"Are you well?" asked Thamarai, trying to change the tack of the conversation.

"What's happening in your class? With that girl?"

"There are so many girls in my class. Sixty-three I think."

"Oh, let's not waste our time asking her questions. I bet she doesn't even know the English Sir has been transferred. Did you know that?"

"Yes," lied Thamarai.

"Get lost. You don't know anything."

"Are you all well?" she asked again.

"Stop asking if we are well," snapped the sisters.

"Okay," she said. "It was nice to see you."

Thamarai quickly made her way into her house. She did not look back, not even when the sisters called after her, demanding that she return.

***

After hot and uneventful holidays, 12th standard finally fell on the erstwhile 11A. It came in a flurry of dummy exam papers, extra tuition classes, and anxiety diarrhoea. Thamarai did not study, but she did take to reading the textbooks as if she was reading a novel. She would start with a certain amount of sleepy bemusement, nod appreciatively at the twists and turns, and then forget all about it once she closed the text. She covered pages and pages of her rough notebook with tiny dashes. She listened to S.T. Priya sing from her many songbooks. She watched Prasanna sometimes, but not very often.

As the sisters had told her, the English Sir had been transferred, starting as a headmaster in a nearby village school in the new academic year. P. Yamuna seemed completely unfazed by this news. Other girls were annoyed that he was leaving the GGHSS for a higher appointment, but they took heart that his new post was at a village school. Village girls were not like small town girls. They would give it back if he tried anything with them. They would not be afraid to beat him with chappals or slap him; some might even bring machetes to school. Nobody could mess with village girls.

The year passed uneventfully. S.T. Priya and P. Yamuna both joined a group of classmates who all studied together, spending hours in the corridor, reciting parts of textbooks to each other like they were praying. Thamarai failed every test or exam she took, even the open-book tests. Many other girls failed too.

Almost everyone had plans for after 12th. There were girls who were planning on spending their days at home or in a relative's house. Others were going to study further, with a few even having the audacity to aspire towards being a doctor or engineer. A number of these girls would fail, but some would succeed.

That year, a few successful akkas came to speak to the class about motivation and the future. One was a doctor and the other was doing something with computers. They talked like everything was possible, and all one had to do was work hard. They were testaments to this. They advised everyone to ask about scholarships and government education schemes. Society was not like it used to be, and there was really no reason why a young woman couldn't achieve great things.

But none of this will happen to me, Thamarai thought to herself. She knew it. The old familiar lump of jealousy appeared and sat heavily in her throat. She had not felt it in some time.

***

Akkas disappear. They may turn into lobster-like creatures that sadly wander the halls of the GGHSS. They may become large, translucent flowers that only bloom in moonlight. They may turn into bobby pins or old handkerchiefs and stay in the GGHSS forever. When P. Yamuna disappeared, it was into a hastily arranged marriage, soon after the 12th exams. She moved with her husband to a neighbouring town and never came back, not even to visit the big temple. The English Sir went on to join a small, local political party and became known as a "social worker". Years later, women of a certain age still referred to him as a porikki, and spoke with anger about how he had grown from strength to strength, despite everything he had done.

After getting first rank at school, Prasanna went to Chennai for college, and finally to America for work. After divorcing her first husband, she met a man called Chuck, and the two of them lived together in a green and expensive neighbourhood. Once, when Chuck asked her about her school life in India, she told him about the English Sir and P. Yamuna and what a terrible scandal it had all been. He struggled to understand why it was so bad to touch a girl's hand, or why girls washed their hair every day during their periods. When Prasanna tried to tell him about Thamarai, she broke down and carried a heavy sadness with her for over a month. Chuck did not understand this either.

S.T. Priya surprised herself by how well she did in the 12th exams. For the first time, her father was proud of her and S.T. Priya never forgot that feeling. She went for teacher's training, got her degree, and became a teacher at the local private school, turning down an offer to work at the GGHSS. She married well and lived comfortably in the same town she was born and raised in. She never spoke of the incident on the Phantom First Floor, though she would often speak of Thamarai, and what a crazy girl she had been. She always spoke about Thamarai in the past tense.

Sometime after 12th standard was over, Thamarai got her period again. The flow was heavy and lasted for weeks, soaking through all of her menstrual rags, even when she wore two or three at once. There were no cramps, but blood kept draining from her, quietly and gently.

One day, Thamarai came to the school office to get her mark certificate. She wore a shabby salwar kameez and kept dropping her cycle key. Nobody remembered her. After her mark sheet had finally been found and signed for, she left the office and collided with a 6th standard girl carrying a small tower of notebooks. Thamarai helped her up, and the 6th standard girl went on her way.

Shortly afterwards, Thamarai went up the school stairs, running up the steps like she was flying.

She never came down again.